PRAISE FOR MURIEL BA
THE ELEGANCE OF THE HEDGEHOG

"This is a novel that celebrates the gut feeling, the inspired moment when life changes forever because of a gesture, a laugh, a step off the pavement, or even a glimpse of a beautiful flower. A warning, though: This story, like all great tales, will break your heart, but it will also make you realize—or remember—that sometimes the pain is worth it, that there's also enough beauty in the world, but only if you see beyond yourself."—*Chicago Sun-Times*

"At one point Madame Michel asks herself, 'What is the purpose of intelligence if it is not to serve others?' What indeed? Certainly, the intelligent Muriel Barbery has served readers well by giving us the gently satirical, exceptionally winning and inevitably bittersweet *Elegance of the Hedgehog*."
—*The Washington Post*

"Astute social satire and abstruse German philosophy are rarely found together, but here they are in this ingenious work of fiction."—*The Boston Globe*

"This dark but redemptive novel, an international bestseller, marks the English debut of Normandy philosophy professor Barbery . . . By turns very funny (particularly in Paloma's sections) and heartbreaking, Barbery never allows either of her dour narrators to get too cerebral or too sentimental. Her simple plot and sudden denouement add up to a great deal more than the sum of their parts."—*Publishers Weekly*

"In this supple novel of ideas, a best-seller in France . . . two autodidacts share an allergy to grammatical errors (the concierge considers a misplaced comma an 'underhanded attack') and a love of tea and moments of ineffable beauty. Barbery's sly wit, which bestows lightness on the most ponderous cogitations, keeps her tale aloft."—*The New Yorker*

"*The Elegance of the Hedgehog* reminded me of *Mrs. Palfrey at the Claremont*, with its sense of renewal near the end of a life and a celebration of the beauty of small moments. It's a quiet, placid-moving book that takes time out to discuss the theory of phenomenology, the function of literature in life, the barrenness of a certain kind of scholarship."—*Christian Science Monitor*

" [*The Elegance of the Hedgehog* tells] a beautiful story with a large cast of fascinating, complicated characters whose behavior is delightfully unpredictable. Maybe the novel's hefty sections on transcendental phenomenology, William of Ockham, and 17th-century Dutch painting discourage readers who just want a good old-fashioned story. Ms. Barbery, who has studied and taught philosophy, seems entirely comfortable mixing the profound with the quotidian, Mozart's *Requiem* with Eminem. No idea is too big or small to find a home in the Parisian apartment building where most of the characters live."—*The Wall Street Journal*

"Barbery is not above ending her tale with a heartbreaking jolt. By then, however, she has drawn us into her Paris microcosm, which seems much less foreign than familiar. Her fable of 'love, friendship and the beauty of Art' not only gives innocence a voice, but also shows what a powerful novel can do: transport, educate and, ultimately, console."—*Toronto Star*

"Despite the topic of suicide and many philosophical ponderings, the Renee and Paloma's narrations are delightfully colorful, idealistic and witty. They are written as if the two are communicating with us in personal journals, speaking with confessional intimacy. The author uses these lovable characters to

express enduring messages about assumptions we make that distort relationships . . . These are the very things you will find in this engaging story that ends surprisingly but with a final message of what life is about. It includes the music of Satie, despair and beauty, and an 'always' within 'never.'"
—NPR's *Day to Day*

"Barbery captures life's small, indeed minuscule, pleasures, those perfect moments in which everything hangs suspended . . . Funny, intelligent, conveyed with a fine, melodious language, this philosophical fairy tale has something of the oriental about it: earnestly buoyant, airy, like a haiku."—*Channel 5* (France)

"Hedgehog or Prozac? At first, the question may seem absurd. But it becomes less so when one learns that a Parisian psychotherapist is prescribing Muriel Barbery's bestselling novel *The Elegance of the Hedgehog* to her patients. 'Yes, I am prescribing it, and I do mean prescribing. This book can do a lot of good . . . [it's] a real toolbox that one can look into to resolve one's problems.' . . . And, indeed, all women, at least once, even Carla Bruni, have lived through the kind of psychological self-denigration that Renée inflicts on herself in the opening scene of the book. The ultimate celebration of every person's invisible part (Renée smells of cabbage soup but reads Husserl) constitutes one of the book's operative factors."
—*L'Express* (France)

"Appearances can be deceptive: this is one of the book's messages. The writing is succinct, unusual, light yet erudite. And the story approaches that of a fable, but without the puerile elements and with a little extra touch of impertinence."
—*Le Figaro* (France)

"The invincible appeal of this book is in its formidably charming characters and in the multitude of intelligent reflections on pets, burnt out cars, learning and scholarship, and much more."—*Nouvel Observateur* (France)

"The concierge [in *The Elegance of the Hedgehog*] is a minor masterpiece à la Simenon, tucked away in her loge with her cat—de rigueur, of course—her 'façade' conforms to convention, but what lies behind the façade astounds."
—*WUZ Magazine* (Italy)

"*The Elegance of the Hedgehog* is about the victory of the defenseless over the self-important, about how difficult it is to endure when situations become extreme. Finally, it is about how you cannot hold anything against art except perhaps for the fact that, though it may appear to suspend time, it does not offer a means of defying mortality."—*Der Spiegel* (Germany)

"This book is as extraordinary as its heroines. Free of any real 'action' it is nonetheless immensely exciting and captivating. For the most part, the book focuses on two intelligent characters who philosophize about the small pleasures of everyday life. But the manner in which they do so is touching, exhilarating, fascinating and entertaining all at the same time—and at times incredibly funny. Whoever is convinced that philosophical discourse is highbrow and boring will think otherwise after having read *The Elegance of the Hedgehog*."
—*Buchenreule* (Germany)

"Great social satire, a very intelligent guide through art and philosophy—a most entertaining and moving story about two outsiders."—*Medien* (Germany)

ALSO BY

MURIEL BARBERY

The Elegance of the Hedgehog

GOURMET RHAPSODY

Muriel Barbery

GOURMET RHAPSODY

*Translated from the French
by Alison Anderson*

Europa
editions

Europa Editions
116 East 16th Street
New York, N.Y. 10003
www.europaeditions.com
info@europaeditions.com

Translation by Alison Anderson
Original title: *Une gourmandise*
Translation copyright © 2009 by Europa Editions

This work has been published thanks to support from
the French Ministry of Culture – Centre National du Livre
Ouvrage publié avec le concours du Ministère
Français chargé de la Culture – Centre National du Livre

Library of Congress Cataloging in Publication Data is available
ISBN 978-1-933372-95-2

Barbery, Muriel
Gourmet Rhapsody

Book design by Emanuele Ragnisco
www.mekkanografici.com

Cover photo © H. Armstrong Roberts/ClassicStock/Corbis

Prepress by Plan.ed – Rome

Printed in Canada

CONTENTS

To Stéphane, without whom . . .

Flavor

Rue de Grenclle, the Bedroom

When I took possession of the table, it was as supreme monarch. We were kings, the suns of those few hours of banqueting, who would determine their futures and describe their horizons—tragically limited or mouth-wateringly distant and radiant—as chefs. I would stride into the room the way a consul entered the arena, and I would give the order for the feast to begin. Those who have never tasted the intoxicating nectar of power cannot imagine the sudden explosion of adrenaline that radiates throughout the body, releasing a harmony of movement, erasing all fatigue, along with any reality that does not bend to the orders of your pleasure; the ecstasy of unbridled power, when one need no longer struggle but merely enjoy the spoils of battle, and savor without cease the headiness that comes with inspiring fear.

That is who we were, and how we reigned as lords and masters over the finest establishments in France, filled with the excellence of the dishes, with our own glory, and with our unquenchable desire—like a hunting dog's first, excited flair—to pronounce upon that excellence.

I am the greatest food critic in the world. It is I who has taken this minor art and raised it to a rank of utmost prestige. Everyone knows my name, from Paris to Rio, Moscow to Brazzaville, Saigon to Melbourne and Acapulco. I have made, and unmade, reputations, and at sumptuous banquets I have been the knowing and merciless *maître d'oeuvre,* expediting to the four corners of the globe the salt or honey of my pen, to newspapers and broadcasts and various forums, where I have been repeatedly invited to discourse upon that which previously had been reserved for a few select specialized journals or intermittent weekly chronicles. I have, for all eternity, pinned to my list of discoveries some of the most prestigious butterflies among practicing chefs. The glory and the demise of Partais, or the fall of Sangerre, or the increasingly incandescent success of Marquet can be attributed to me alone. For all eternity, indeed, I have made them what they are; for all eternity.

I have held eternity under the skin of my words, and tomorrow I shall die. I shall die in forty-eight hours— unless I have been dying for sixty-eight years and it is only today that I have deigned to notice. Whatever the case may be, the verdict was handed down yesterday by my friend the physician Chabrot: "Old boy, you've got forty-eight hours." How ironic! After decades of grub, deluges of wine and alcohol of every sort, after a life spent in butter, cream, rich sauces, and oil in constant, knowingly orchestrated and meticulously cajoled excess, my trustiest right-hand men, Sir Liver and his associate Stomach, are doing marvelously well and it is my heart that is giving out. I am dying of a cardiac insufficiency. What a bitter pill to swallow! So often have I reproached others for a lack of heart in their cuisine, in their art, that never for a moment did I think that I might be the one lacking therein, this heart now betraying me so brutally, with scarcely concealed disdain, so quickly has the blade been sharpened . . .

I am going to die, but that is of no importance. Since yesterday, since Chabrot, only one thing matters. I am going to die and there is a flavor that has been teasing my taste buds and my heart and I simply cannot recall it. I know that this particular flavor is the first and ultimate truth of my entire life, and that it holds the key to a heart that I have since silenced. I know that it is a flavor from childhood or adolescence, an original, marvelous dish that predates my vocation as a critic, before I had any desire or pretension to expound on my pleasure in eating. A forgotten flavor, lodged in my deepest self, and which has surfaced at the twilight of my life as the only truth ever told—or realized. I search, and cannot find.

Rue de Grenelle, the Concierge's Loge

A nd now what?
    Is it not enough for them that every day the Good
Lord gives us I clean up the muck that falls from
their rich people's shoes, I vacuum the dust they stir up
during their rich people's deambulations, I listen to their
rich people's conversations and concerns, I feed their
mutts, their cats, water their plants, wipe the noses of their
offspring, accept their yearly gifts of money—and that is
indeed the only moment when they don't play at being
rich—I sniff their perfume, I open the door to their relatives, I hand out their mail dripping with bank statements
regarding their rich-people accounts and investments and
overdrafts, I force myself to smile in response to their rich-
people smiles, and, finally, I live in their rich-people building, me, the concierge, a nobody-at-all, a thing behind a
window that people say hello to in great haste to ease their
conscience, because it's awkward, isn't it, to see that old
thing lurking in her dark little hole without any crystal
chandeliers, without any patent-leather slippers, without
any camel's-hair overcoat, it's awkward but at the same
time it's reassuring, like some incarnation of the social dif-
ferences that justify the superiority of their class, like an
ugly thing exalting their munificence, like a foil enhancing
their elegance—no, all that is not enough, because in addi-

tion to all that, in addition to leading this existence as an unbecoming recluse day after day, hour after hour, minute after minute, and what's worst of all, year after year, I am expected to *understand* their rich-people's sorrows?

If they want to have news of the Mââââître, let them ring at *his* bell.

The Man of Property

Rue de Grenelle, the Bedroom

If I go back to my earliest memories, I find that I have always liked eating. I cannot pinpoint exactly my first gastronomic ecstasies, but there is no doubt as to the identity of my first preferred cook: my own grandmother. On the menu for celebrations there was meat in gravy, potatoes in gravy, and the wherewithal to mop up all that gravy. I never knew, subsequently, whether it was my childhood or the stews themselves that I was unable to re-experience, but never again have I sampled as fervently (I am the specialist of such oxymorons) as at my grandmother's table the likes of those potatoes: bursting with gravy, delectable little sponges. Might the forgotten taste throbbing in my breast be hidden somewhere in there? Might it suffice to ask Anna to let a few tubers marinate in the juices of a good traditional *coq au vin?* Alas, I know only too well that it would not. I know that what I am searching for is something that has always eluded my talents, my memory, my consideration. Extravagant *pots-au-feu, poulets chasseur* to make one faint, dizzying *coqs au vin*, astounding *blanquettes*—you have all been the companions of my carnivorous and saucy childhood. I cherish you, amiable casseroles with your fragrance of game—but you are not what I am seeking in this moment.

Despite those early, always faithful, love affairs, in later years my tastes turned to other culinary destinations, and with the additional delight occasioned by the certainty of my own eclecticism, my love of the stew came to be replaced by the urgent call of more austere sensations. The soft, delicate touch on the palate of one's first sushi no longer holds any secrets for me, and I bless the day my tongue discovered the intoxicating, almost erotic, velvet-smooth caress of an oyster slipping in after a chunk of bread smeared with salted butter. I have dissected the magical delicacy of the oyster with such brilliance and finesse that the divine mouthful has become a religious act for all. Between these two extremes—the rich warmth of a daube and the clean crystal of shellfish, I have covered the entire range of culinary art, for I am an encyclopedic esthete who is always one dish ahead of the game—but always one heart behind.

I can hear Paul and Anna speaking in hushed voices in the corridor. I peer through my eyelids. My gaze, as usual, encounters the perfect curve of a sculpture by Fanjol, a birthday present from Anna on my sixtieth birthday; it seems such a long time ago. Paul comes quietly into the room. Of all my nephews and nieces, he is he only one I love and respect, the only one whose presence I can tolerate during the final hours of my life. Therefore, before I can no longer speak at all, I have taken him—along with my wife—into my confidence regarding my distress.

"A dish? A dessert?" asked Anna, with a sob in her voice.

I cannot bear to see her like this. I love my wife, as I have always loved the beautiful objects in my life. That is the way it is. I have lived as a man of property, and I shall

die as one, with neither qualms nor sentimental indulgence; nor do I regret having accumulated property or
having conquered souls and beings as if I were acquiring
an expensive painting. A work of art has a soul. It cannot
be reduced to a simple mineral existence, to the lifeless
elements of which it consists. Perhaps because I know this
I have never felt the least bit ashamed of considering Anna
the most beautiful work of all—this woman who for forty
years has used her finely chiseled beauty and her dignified
tenderness to enliven the chambers of my realm.

I do not like to see her cry. On the threshold of my
death I feel that she is waiting for something, that she suf-
fers for the imminent end looming on the horizon of the
coming hours, and that she is dreading I might disappear
into the same void, bereft of communication, that we have
maintained since our wedding—it is the same void, but
definitive now, without appeal or hope, the false promises
that tomorrow will, perhaps, be another day. I know that
she is thinking or feeling all of this, but that is not what
worries me. We have nothing to say to each other, she and
I, and she will have to accept that things are just as I have
wished them. All I want is for her to understand that that
is the way it is, to appease her suffering and, above all, my
displeasure.

Nothing except that flavor I am pursuing in the limbo
of my memory is of any importance now: enraged by a
betrayal I cannot even recall, it continues to resist me, and
stubbornly slips away.

Rue de Grenelle, the Stairway

I remember our holidays in Greece when we were children, on Tinos—a horrid island, bare and scorched, that I hated from the moment I saw it, from the moment we set foot on solid ground, from the moment we left the gangplank of the ship, the moment we left the winds of the Aegean behind . . .

A big gray and white cat had leapt onto the terrace and from there onto the low wall that separated our villa from the neighbors' invisible house. A big cat: by the standards of the country, he was impressive. The neighborhood abounded in scrawny creatures with bobbing heads and it broke my heart to see them dragging their exhausted bodies around. This cat, however, seemed to have grasped the principles of survival: he had made it past the terrace, gotten as far as the door to the dining room, and once inside the house grew bold and shamelessly swept down like some avenging angel upon the roast chicken that was resting in state upon the table. We found him comfortably indulging in our victuals, not the least bit intimidated, or perhaps just enough to enchant, in the time it took to grab a wing with a smart, expert snap of his teeth and to sneak off through the French doors, his loot in his chops, with a perfunctory growl to the delight of our childhood selves.

Of course, *he* wasn't there. He would be coming back

from Athens a few days later, and we'd tell him the story—Maman would tell him the story, oblivious to his scornful expression or his absence of love—he would pay no attention, he already had his mind on his next feast, far away, at the ends of the earth—without us. All the same, he would look at me with a glint of disappointment in the depths of his eyes, unless it was repulsion, or perhaps cruelty—perhaps all three at the same time—and say, "That is how to survive, that cat is a living lesson," and his words would ring like a bell, words meant to hurt, words meant to wound, to torture the frightened little girl I was, so weak and insignificant: without importance.

He was a brutal man. Brutal in his gestures, in the dominating way he had of grabbing hold of things, his smug laugh, his raptor's gaze. I never saw him *relax*: everything was a pretext for tension. Already at breakfast, on those rare days when he deigned to grace us with his presence, our martyrdom began. The stage was set for psychodrama, he would splutter and expostulate: for the survival of the Empire was at stake, what were we having for lunch? Trips to the market were opportunities for hysteria. My mother bowed to his will, as usual, as always. And then off he would go again, to other restaurants, other women, other vacations, without us, where we were not even—of this I am sure—cause for memories; perhaps, just as he was leaving, we were like flies to him, unwanted flies that you brush away with a sweep of your hand so you needn't think about them anymore. We were his coleopterous insects.

It was one evening; he was walking ahead of us, past the little tourist boutiques in Tinos's only shopping street, with his imperious gait, his hands in his pockets, mindful of no one. The earth could have collapsed beneath our feet, it was all the same to him; he strode ahead and it was up to our little terrorized children's legs to close the chasm between us. We did not yet know that this was the last vacation he would spend with us. The following summer it was with relief—with frenzied delight—that we greeted the news that he wouldn't be coming with us. But we quickly had to resign ourselves to another affliction, that of Maman wandering like a ghost through the places we were meant to enjoy. It struck us as worse than ever because by his very absence he managed to hurt us even more. But on the day I'm remembering, he was very much present and he was climbing up the hill at a discouraging rate—I had just stopped outside a humble little neon-lit restaurant with my hand to my waist, plagued by a cramp. My sides heaving, I was trying to catch my breath when I saw with terror that he was making his way back down to me, followed by Jean, who was livid and gazed at me with big tearful eyes; I stopped breathing. He walked by without seeing me, strode into the little greasy spoon, greeted the proprietor, and while we stood uncertain on the threshold, hopping from one foot to the other he pointed to something behind the counter, raised a hand with his fingers well spread to indicate "three," and motioned briefly to us to enter as he made his way to a table at the far side of the bar.

They were *loukoumades*, perfectly round little fritters that are dropped into boiling oil just long enough for the outside to become crisp while the inside stays tender and cottony; they are then covered in honey and served very hot on a little plate, with a fork and a tall glass of water.

You see, nothing changes. I think the way he does. Just like him, I dissect each sensation in succession; like him, I cloak them with adjectives, dilate them, stretch them over the length of a sentence, or a verbal melody, and I let nothing of the actual food remain, only these magician's words, which will make the readers believe they have been eating as we did . . . Not for nothing am I his daughter . . .

He tasted a fritter, made a face, pushed his plate back and watched us. Although I couldn't see him I sensed that Jean, next to me, was having a terrible time swallowing; whereas I was postponing the moment when I would have to take another bite and, petrified, I gave him a stupid look, for he was studying us.

"Do you like them?" he asked, in his grating voice.

Panic and disorientation. Next to me Jean was breathing quietly. I forced myself.

"Yes," I muttered timidly.

"Why?" he pursued, his tone increasingly dry, but I could see that in the depth of his eyes, which were actually inspecting me for the first time in years, there was a new spark, something I had never seen, like a little speck of caution and hope, inconceivable, harrowing and paralyzing, because for so long I had been accustomed to his not expecting a thing from me.

"Because it's good?" I ventured, hunching my shoulders.

I had lost. How many times since then have I relived in my mind—and in images—this wrenching episode, the moment when something could have shifted, when the bleakness of my fatherless childhood might have been transformed into a new and brilliant love . . . As if in slow motion, against the painful backdrop of my disappointed desire, the seconds tick by; the question, the answer, the waiting, and then the annihilation. The gleam in his eyes is extinguished as quickly as it flared. Disgusted, he turns away, pays, and I am once again relegated to the solitary confinement of his indifference.

But what am I doing here in this stairway, with my pounding heart, rehashing these horrible memories I left behind so long ago—or which should have been left behind, should have subsided after so many years of necessary suffering on the shrink's couch, of being attentive to my own words and conquering each day a bit more of the right to be something other than hatred and terror, the right just to be myself. Laura. His daughter . . . No. I won't go. I've already mourned the father I didn't have.

Meat

Rue de Grenelle, the Bedroom

We left the ship amidst the crowds, noise, dust and general weariness. It had taken two exhausting days to cross Spain, but that was already nothing more than a ghost lingering on the frontier of memory. Sticky, worn out by miles of hazardous roads, displeased with the hasty roadside stops and the barely edible restaurant food, crushed by the heat in the crowded car, which was at last slowly making its way along the pier, we were still living for a short while longer in the world of travel, but already we could sense the splendor of arrival.

Tangiers. Where many a passage has ended and many a new journey has begun. With its vigorous port, its embarkations and disembarkations—perhaps the most powerful city on earth. Halfway between Madrid and Casablanca, she is a formidable town that, unlike Algeciras on the other side of the straits, has avoided becoming merely a port town. Consistent, instantly itself despite its piers gaping open onto elsewhere, an enclave of the senses at a crossroads. Tangiers instantly seized hold of us with its vigor. Our journey was nearly over. And although our final destination was Rabat, the town that was the cradle of my mother's family and where, since the return to France, we spent every summer, we always felt, as soon as we reached

Tangiers, that we had arrived. We would park the car outside the Hotel Bristol, modest but clean, on a steep street
that led to the medina. A shower and then later, on foot,
we would make our way to the theater of succulence foretold.

It was at the entrance to the medina. Arrayed beneath
the arcades on the square, a number of small kebab restaurants greeted passers-by. We walked into "our" restaurant
and went up to the second floor: a huge table took all the
space in the narrow room whose walls were painted blue
and which looked out over the circular piazza below; we
would sit down, our stomachs tight and eager in anticipa-
tion of the unchanging set menu that was just waiting
upon our pleasure. A pitiful but conscientious fan gave the
room the charm of a breezy space but did little to refresh
us; the harried waiter set down on the sticky Formica some
glasses and a carafe of iced water. My mother would order
in perfect Arabic. Scarcely five minutes passed before the
dishes were there on the table.

Perhaps I shall not find what I am looking for. I will, at
least, have had the opportunity to recall this: the grilled
meat, the mechouia salad, the mint tea and the *cornes de
gazelle*. I was Ali Baba. The cave of treasures: this was it,
the perfect rhythm, the shimmering harmony between
portions, each one exquisite unto itself, but verging on the
sublime by virtue of the strict, ritual succession. The meat-
balls, grilled with the utmost respect for their firmness,
had lost none of their succulence during their passage
through fire, and filled my professionally carnivorous
mouth with a thick, warm, spicy, juicy wave of masticatory
pleasure. The sweet bell peppers, unctuous and fresh, soft-

ened my taste buds already subjugated by the virile rigor of the meat, and prepared them for the next powerful assault. Everything was there in abundance. From time to time we would take a sip of that carbonated water you can also find in Spain but which seems to have no real equivalent in France: a stinging, insolent, invigorating water, neither bland nor too bubbly. When at last we were sated and somewhat dazed, we would shove our plates away and look in vain for a back to the bench so that we might relax; the waiter brought the tea, poured it according to the established ritual, and on the table, which had been only haphazardly wiped clean, he set down a plate of sugar-covered crescents, the *cornes de gazelle*. No one was the least bit hungry anymore, but that is precisely what is so good about the moment devoted to pastries: they can only be appreciated to the full extent of their subtlety when they are not eaten to assuage our hunger, when the orgy of their sugary sweetness is not destined to fill some primary need but to coat our palate with all the benevolence of the world.

If my quest today is to lead me somewhere, no doubt it will not be far from this quintessence of civilization, the extraordinary contrast between the pungency of a simple, powerful piece of meat and the knowing tenderness of a sweet and utterly superfluous delicacy. The entire history of humanity, of our tribe of sensitive predators, can be summed up in these meals in Tangiers, and in retrospect this is why they had such an uncommon power to exhilarate.

I shall never return to that beautiful maritime metropolis, where you arrive in the port, the long hoped-for refuge during the storm—never again. But what do I care? I am on the road to my redemption. And it is far from the beaten path, along a road where the nature of our human condition can be truly felt, in a place far from the luxurious banquets of my career as a critic and the attendant prestige, that I must now seek the instrument of my liberation.

(Georges)

Rue de Provence

T he first time was at Marquet's. You should have seen it, you ought to have witnessed it at least once in your life—the way this huge feline would take possession of the room, his leonine majesty, the royal nod in greeting the maître d', be it as a regular, a distinguished guest, or a proprietor. He remains standing, almost in the middle of the room, conversing with Marquet, who has just come out of her den, the kitchen; he places his hand on her shoulder as they make their way to his table. There are many people around them, speaking loudly, they are all splendid with a combination of arrogance and grace but you can tell that they are watching him on the sly, that they are resplendent in his shadow, that they are hanging on his every word. He is the Maître and, surrounded the stars of his retinue, he disposes, while they merely chatter.

The maître d' had to whisper in his ear, "One of your young colleagues is here today, Sir." He turned toward me, observed me for a brief moment during which I felt as if I were being X-rayed right through to my deepest mediocrities, and then he turned away. Almost immediately I was summoned to join him at his table.

It was a master class, one of those days when he put on the garments of the spiritual guide and invited all the finest young food critics in Europe to dine with him, and like a pontiff gone back to mere preaching, from the height of his pulpit he taught the trade to a few bedazzled disciples. The Pope sitting enthroned among his cardinals: there was indeed something of a great ceremonial mass about this gastronomic council, where he reigned supreme over a hushed, contemplative elite. The rules were simple. You ate, you commented as you liked, he listened, the verdict fell. I was paralyzed. Like an ambitious but shy fellow who is introduced for the first time to the Godfather, or a young man from the provinces at his first Parisian soirée; like a besotted admirer who encounters his Diva by chance, or a little shoemaker whose gaze meets that of the Princess, or a young author entering the temple of publishing for the first time: like them, I was petrified. He was the Christ and, at that particular Last Supper, I was Judas—not that I wanted to betray him, merely that I was an impostor, lost on Olympian heights, invited by mistake, and whose paltry blandness would, at any moment, be revealed in broad daylight. I was silent throughout the entire meal and he did not call upon me, keeping the whip or the caress of his decrees for his herd of regular followers. At dessert, however, he did question me, in silence. Everyone was glossing unsuccessfully over a scoop of orange sorbet.

Unsuccessfully. All criteria are subjective. Something that when measured by common sense might seem magical and masterful will fracture pathetically when faced with the sheer rock face of genius. Their conversation was dizzying; the art of speaking supplanted the art of tasting. They all promised, to a man—by virtue of the mastery and precision of their commentary, and the dazzling skill of their practiced tirades, which penetrated the sorbet with brilliant syntax and poetic flashes—to become masters of culinary expression one day, for if they were still in the shadow of their elder's aura, this would only be temporary. Meanwhile the uneven, almost lumpy orange sphere continued to liquefy in our plates, its silent avalanche reflecting something of his disapproval. For nothing met with his approval.

Irritated, on the verge of extreme bad temper or even self-incrimination for having allowed himself to be shackled with such pathetic company . . . his tenebrous gaze catches hold of mine, inviting me . . . I clear my throat, quaking and pink with confusion, because the sorbet does indeed inspire many things, but not the sort of things one ought to say here, at this concert of high-flying phraseologists, amidst these orchestra seats filled with culinary strategists, confronted with this living genius with his immortal pen and fiery gaze. And yet now I must—I must say something, and right away, because his entire person is emanating impatience and irritation. Therefore I clear my throat once again, moisten my lips, and step off into the void.

"It reminds me of the sorbets my grandmother used to make . . . "

On the face of the infatuated young man sitting across from me I see an incipient smile of mockery, his cheeks starting slowly to expand with the mirth that will explode into lethal laughter, and ready to give me a first-class burial: good evening, goodbye, dear sir, you came, you won't come again, a good night to you.

But *he* is smiling at me with a warmth one would not have thought him capable of: a broad, frank smile, the smile of a wolf but meant from one wolf to another in the complicity of the pack, friendly, relaxed, something like, hello friend, it's good to find you here. And he says, "So tell me, then, about your grandmother."

It is an invitation, but also a veiled threat. While his request may seem kindly, it is weighted with the obligation for me to perform and the danger that after such a fine beginning I might disappoint him. My reply was a pleasant surprise to him, for it was in stark contrast to the bravura passages of the virtuoso soloists, and he liked that. For the time being.

"My grandmother's cooking . . . " I say, searching desperately for my words, for the decisive formula that will justify both my reply and my art—my talent.

But most unexpectedly he comes to my rescue.

"Would you believe"—and he smiles to me, almost affectionately—"I also had a grandmother, whose kitchen was a magic cave for me. I think that my entire career sprang from the fumets and aromas that came from that kitchen and which filled me, as a child, with desire. I literally went mad with desire. People don't really know what desire is, true desire, when it hypnotizes you and takes hold of your entire soul, surrounds it utterly, in such a way that you become demented, possessed, ready to do anything for a tiny crumb, for a whiff of whatever is being concocted there beneath your nostrils, subjugated by the devil's own perfume! And my grandmother was overflowing with energy and a scathing good humor, a prodigious life force that suffused her entire kitchen with a sort of brilliant vitality, and it was as if I were at the heart of some molten matter: she radiated, and enveloped me in this warm and fragrant radiance!"

"With me, it was an impression rather of entering the temple," I say, relieved, in possession now of the strength of my intuition and thus of my argumentation (I let out a long inward sigh). "My grandmother was not so cheerful and radiant, far from it. She embodied rather the character of austere, submissive dignity. Protestant to the tips of her fingers, only ever cooking calmly and painstakingly, without passion or thrills, an affair of white porcelain platters and soup tureens that came to a table filled with silent guests, who without haste or visible emotion consumed dishes that could have made you burst with joy and delight."

"How odd," he says to me, "I have always attributed the success and magic of her good-natured, tasty cooking to her easy temperament and southern sensuality. I even thought at times that it was her stupidity and lack of education and culture that had made her an accomplished cook, and that all the energy which did not nourish her mind was free to nourish her fair."

"No," I say after a moment's reflection, "what went into their art was neither their personality nor their gift for life, any more than it was the simplicity of their spirit, their love of a job well done, or their austerity. I think they were aware, without even telling themselves as much, that they were accomplishing a noble task, one at which they could excel and that was subordinate, material, or basely utilitarian in appearance only. They knew well enough that, beyond all the humiliations they had suffered not in their own name but by virtue of their condition as women, that when their men came home and sat down at the table, their own reign, as women, would begin. And it wasn't some sort of stranglehold they had over their 'economy of the interior,' where they would, as sovereigns in their own right, take revenge on the power that the men had over the 'exterior.' It was a great deal more than that; they knew that their exploits spoke directly to the hearts and the bodies of their men, and that in the eyes of those men this conferred upon the women a power greater than that which the women themselves attributed to male intrigues of power and money or all the compelling arguments of society. They held their men not by the ties of domestic administration, or through children or respectability or even those of the bedroom, but by their taste buds, and this was as sure a thing as if they had put them into a cage into which the men had rushed of their own volition."

He is listening to me very attentively and I am learning to recognize in him the quality—so rare among men of power—that enables one to determine where the display—the conversation allowing each participant to mark his territory and show signs of power—ends, and the true dialogue begins. Around us, however, things are falling apart. The presumptuous young fellow who only a moment ago was so eager to assail me with his mockery now has a waxy complexion and a vacant stare. The others remain silent, at the edge of an abyss of desolation. I continue.

"What did they feel, those men—so full of themselves, those 'heads' of the family, trained from the dawn of time, in a patriarchal society, to become the masters—when they took their first bite of those simple yet extraordinary dishes that their wives had prepared in their private laboratories? What does a man experience when his tongue—which, up to this point, has been saturated with spices, sauces, meat, cream, and salt—is suddenly refreshed by contact with a slow avalanche of ice and fruit that is ever so slightly rustic, and ever so slightly lumpy; thus, what was ephemeral is now slightly less so, slowed by the more sluggish deliquescence of fruity little chunks of ice gently breaking apart . . . Quite simply, those men experienced paradise, and even if they could not admit it to themselves, they knew very well that they were incapable of offering it to their wives in return, because for all their empires and arrogance, they could never make their women swoon the way those women made them swoon—with an orgasmic experience via the taste buds."

He interrupts me without brutality.

"It's very interesting," he says, "I see exactly what you mean. But in this instance you are explaining talent through injustice, our grandmothers' gift through their condition as oppressed women—although there have been many great cooks who suffered neither from an inferiority of caste nor a life deprived of prestige or power. How do you reconcile this with your theory?"

"No chef can cook, nor has ever cooked, the way our grandmothers did. All the factors we have been evoking here"—and I place a slight emphasis on the "we" to clearly point out that at this point I am the one who is officiating—"have produced a very specific cuisine, that of women in their homes, within the enclosure of their private interior: a cuisine which sometimes might lack refinement, which always contains a 'home-cooked' side to it, that is, solid and nourishing, made to stick to your ribs,—but which is basically and above all intensely sensual: we understand that when we talk about 'flesh' it is no mere coincidence that it evokes both the pleasures of the table and those of love. After all it was through their cooking that they lured, and seduced, and charmed—and that is what inspired it and made it like no other."

Again he smiles to me. Then in front of all his crestfallen epigones—devastated because they fail to understand, *cannot* understand that despite performing their gastronomic balancing act, despite erecting temples to the glory of the goddess Grub, they have been upstaged by a wretched mongrel pup who came along with his gnawed yellow old bone in his sheepish muzzle, and who now sits here before them while they mourn—he says to me, "So that we might quietly continue this fascinating discussion, would you do me the honor of joining me for lunch tomorrow at Lessière's?"

I called Anna some time ago and I understood that I would not be going. Not now. Not ever. This is the end of an epic tale, the story of my coming of age, which, like in the novels of the same description, went from wonder to ambition, from ambition to disillusion, and from disillusion to cynicism. The rather shy, sincere young man I once was has become a very influential critic—feared, respected, educated at the best school and welcomed in the best circles. But with each passing day and well ahead of time, he feels older and older, increasingly weary, increasingly useless: a clattering man, old before his time, full of venom as he trots out the better part of a self which is inexorably crumbling away and portends nothing better than twilight years spent as a lucid, pitiful old bastard. And is that what he is feeling now? Is that what would steal secretly under his somewhat weary eyelids with a hint of sadness, a pinch of nostalgia? Shall I follow in his footsteps, experiencing the same regret, the same erring ways? Or am I just in a phase of feeling sorry for myself—since I am far, so far, from the brilliance of his private peregrinations? I shall never know.

The king is dead. Long live the king.

Fish

Ruc de Grenelle, the Bedroom

Every summer we returned to Brittany. It was still the era when school did not start again until mid-September; my grandparents, who had recently made their fortune, rented a large villa on the coast, at the end of the season, and the entire family would gather there. It was a miraculous time. I was not yet old enough to understand that these simple people, who had worked hard all their lives and upon whom fate had smiled somewhat late in life, had decided that, rather than keep their money, as others might have done, under their woolen mattress, they would spend it with their family and in their lifetime. I was, however, already aware that we children were being pampered, albeit in an intelligent way that still astonishes me, for I only ever knew how to spoil my own children—spoil in the strictest sense of the term. I caused them to rot and decompose, those three children who emerged from my wife's entrails, gifts I had negligently given to her in exchange for her decorative wifely abnegation—terrible gifts, when I think about it today, for what are children other than the monstrous excrescences of our own selves, pitiful substitutes for our unfulfilled desires? For the likes of me—people, in other words, who already have something which gives them pleasure in life—children are worthy of interest only when they finally leave home and become something other than one's own daughters or sons. I do not love them, I have never loved them, and I feel no remorse on that account. If they expend all their energy hating me with all their strength, that is no concern of mine; the only paternity that I might lay claim to is that of my own oeuvre. And the buried flavor that I cannot find is beginning to make me doubt even that.

As for my grandparents, they loved us in their way: undividedly. They had made their own children into an assortment of neuropaths and degenerates: a melancholy son, a hysterical daughter, another daughter who committed suicide, and finally my own father who escaped madness at the cost of all fantasy, and who chose a wife in his own image; what safeguarded my parents was the way they applied their apathy and mediocrity to protecting themselves from excess—from the abyss, in other words. And I was the only ray of sunlight in my mother's existence: I was her god, and a god I have remained; I have preserved nothing of her sad face or her lifeless cooking or her somewhat plaintive voice, but I have preserved all her love, which endowed me with the self-assurance of a king. To have been adulated by one's mother . . . Thanks to her I have conquered empires, I have confronted life with an irresistible brutality which opened to me the gates of glory. The child who had everything has become a man without pity, thanks to the love of a shrew who, in the end, was resigned to gentleness solely by her lack of ambition.

With their grandchildren, on the other hand, my grandparents were the most charming of individuals. Deep in their souls they had a talent for the sort of good-natured and mischievous behavior that had been restrained by their burden as parents, but as grandparents, they could

give it free rein. The summer radiated freedom. Everything seemed possible in our world of fervid exploration,
of joyful, pseudo-secret outings on the rocks by the beach
at nightfall; anything could happen, given the unprecedented generosity that extended invitations to all the
neighbors at random on those summer days. My grandmother officiated at the stove with a haughty tranquility.
She weighed over two hundred pounds, had a mustache,
laughed like a man and barked at us with all the grace of a
truck driver whenever we ventured into the kitchen. Yet
under the influence of her expert hands, the most banal
substances were transformed into miracles of faith. White
wine flowed freely and we ate and ate and ate. Sea urchins,
oysters, mussels, grilled shrimp, shellfish with mayonnaise,
calamari in sauce, but also ("You can't change who you
are!") daubes, blanquettes, paellas, and poultry—roasted,
stewed or à la crème; we were showered with food.

Once a month my grandfather would put on a strict
and solemn expression at breakfast, then get up without a
word and head off alone to the fish market. Then we knew
that *the* day had come. My grandmother would raise her
eyes to the heavens, mumble that "as per usual the whole
house will stink for ages," and mutter something rude
about her husband's culinary talents. I personally felt
moved to tears at the thought of what was to follow, and I
may have known that she was joking, but I nevertheless
fleetingly begrudged her the fact that she did not incline
her head with humility in this sacred moment. An hour
later my grandfather returned from the port with an enormous crate smelling of the sea. He sent us off to the
beach—we were the "brats," and we would head off all
atremble with excitement, already home again in our

thoughts but docile and mindful not to go against our grandfather's wishes. When we set off for home at one o'clock, after what was at best a distracted swim, so hopelessly did we anticipate the prospect of lunch, we could already catch a whiff of the heavenly aroma from the corner of the street. I could have sobbed for joy.

The grilled sardines filled the entire neighborhood with their ashy marine aroma. A thick gray smoke rose from the thujas that surrounded the garden. The men from the neighboring houses came to lend my grandpa a hand. On enormous grills the little silvery fish were already turning crisp in the noon breeze. There was laughter and talk, and bottles of well-chilled dry white wine were opened; the men sat down at last and the women came out of the kitchen with their piles of immaculate plates. My grandmother reached skillfully for a plump little fish, sniffed its perfume, and dropped it on the plate with a few others. With her big moist cow eyes she looked at me kindly and said, "Here, little fella, the first lot's for you! Good heavens, but doesn't he just love 'em, that boy!" And everyone burst out laughing, and slapped me on the back while the prodigious sustenance was placed before me. I did not hear another thing. My eyes open wide, I stared at the object of my desire: the gray, blistered skin, with its long black stripes that no longer even clung to the flesh it was covering. My knife slipped into the fish's spine and carefully divided the whitish meat: it was perfectly cooked, and came off in firm little strips without the least resistance.

In the flesh of grilled fish, from the humblest of mackerel to the most refined salmon, there is something that defies culture. Early man, in learning to cook fish, must have felt his humanity for the first time, in this substance where fire revealed both essential purity and wildness. To say that the flesh is delicate, that its taste is both subtle and expansive, that it stimulates the gums with a mixture of sharpness and sweetness; to say that the combination of the grilled skin's faint bitterness and the extreme smoothness of the firm, strong, harmonious flesh, filling one's mouth with a flavor from elsewhere, elevates the grilled sardine to the rank of culinary apotheosis, is at best like evoking the soporific virtues of opium. For what is at issue here is neither how delicate or sweet or strong or smooth the grilled sardine may be, but its wild nature. One must be strong in spirit to confront a taste like this; concealed within, very precisely, is the primitive brutality that forges our humanity when we come into contact with it. And one must be pure in spirit, as well, a spirit that knows how to chew with vigor, to the exclusion of any other food: I scorned the potatoes and salted butter which my grandmother had set out next to my plate, and devoured relentlessly the strips of fish.

Meat is virile, powerful; fish is strange and cruel. It comes from another world, a secret ocean that will never yield to us; it bears witness to the absolute relativity of our existence, and yet it offers itself to us through the ephemeral revelation of unknown realms. When I was savoring these grilled sardines, like an autistic child whom nothing could trouble at that point in time, I knew that this extraordinary confrontation with a sensation from elsewhere was making me human, bringing its contrasting nature to bear to teach me my human essence. Infinite, cruel, primitive, refined ocean: between our avid teeth we seize the products of your mysterious activity. The grilled sardine suffused my palate with its frank and exotic bouquet, with each mouthful I grew more mature, and every time my tongue caressed the marine ash of blistered skin I felt exulted.

But that is not what I have been looking for, either. I have brought to my memory forgotten sensations buried beneath the magnificence of my regal banquets; I have become reacquainted with the early stages of my vocation; I have exhumed the effluvia of my childhood soul. And that is not it. Time is pressing, and brings with it the uncertain yet terrifying contours of my ultimate failure. I do not want to give up. I am making an immoderate effort to remember. And what if, in the long run, the thing that is taunting me is not even tasty? Like Proust's abominable madeleine, that oddity of a pastry reduced one sinister and drab afternoon into a spoonful of spongy crumbs— supreme offense—in a cup of herbal tea, in actual fact my memory may merely be associated with some mediocre dish, and it is only the emotion attached to it that remains precious, and that might reveal to me a gift for living that I had not previously understood.

(Jean)

Café des Amis, 18th Arrondissement

Purulent old goatskin. Putrid rotting carcass. Die, just go ahead and die. Die in your silk sheets, in your pasha's bed, in your bourgeois cage, die, die, die. At least then we'll have your money, even if we'll never have your favor. All your big-shot foodie money can't do you an ounce of good anymore, so it will go to other people, your rich landlord money, the cash from your corruption, your parasitical activities, all that food, all that luxury, such a waste . . . Die . . . Everyone is rushing to your side—Maman, Maman who really should leave you to die alone, abandon you the way you abandoned her, but she won't, she stays there, inconsolable, and she really believes she is losing everything. I'll never get it, why she's so blind, so resigned, and how she manages to convince herself that she has had the life she wanted, her vocation as a holy martyr; shit, it makes me want to puke, Maman, Maman . . . And then there's that dickhead Paul, with his airs of the prodigal son, his spiritual heir hypocrisy, he must be crawling all over the bed, do you need a cushion, Uncle, would you like me to read you a few pages of Proust, or Dante, or Tolstoy? I can't stand that guy, that piece of trash, Mr. Perfect Bourgeois with his distinguished gentlemanly airs, screwing the whores on the rue Saint-Denis; I've seen him, yes I've seen him coming out of a house over there . . . Oh, but what's the use, huh, what's the use of stirring all this up, stirring up my ugly duckling bitterness, it will only prove the old man right: my children are imbeciles, that's what he used to say, quite calmly, in our presence, we were all embarrassed, except him, of course, he couldn't even see what might be *shocking,* not just about saying it but even thinking it! My children are imbeciles, especially my son. He'll never amount to anything. No you're wrong, father, they have amounted to something, your brats, they are nothing more than your own creation, you chopped them up fine and spat them out and drowned them in a stinking gravy and that is what they have become: weaklings, losers, failures, sludge. And yet! And yet you could have made them gods, your kids. I remember how proud I used to feel when I would go out with you, when you would take me to the market or the restaurant; I was just a little tyke and you were so tall, with your big warm hand holding tight to mine, and your profile, when I saw it from below, the profile of an emperor, and your lion's mane! You had such a proud look and I was over the moon, over the moon to have a father like you . . . And now here I am, sobbing, my voice is breaking, my heart is broken, crushed; I hate you, I love you, and I hate my own ambivalence so much I could scream, fucking ambivalence that has ruined my life, because I am still your son, because I've never been anything other than the son of a monster!

The real ordeal is not leaving those you love but learning to live without those who don't love you. And my sorry life has been spent longing so ardently for all the love you have withheld, your absent love, oh for Christ's sake, is this the best I can do, weeping over my miserable fate as a poor unloved little boy? There are far more important things,

I'm going to die soon, too, and no one gives a damn, and I don't give a damn either, I don't give a damn because, right now, he is dying and I love the bastard, I love him, oh shit . . .

The Vegetable Garden

Rue de Grenelle, the Bedroom

My aunt Marthe's house was a dilapidated old place buried in ivy, and because of its façade with one bricked-in window, there was something distinctly one-eyed about the place that perfectly suited both its surroundings and its occupant. Aunt Marthe, the eldest of my mother's sisters and the only one who did not inherit a nickname, was a sour, ugly, malodorous old maid who lived between her chicken coop and her rabbit hutches in unbelievable squalor. Indoors, as was to be expected, there was neither running water, electricity, telephone nor television. But above all, beyond this lack of creature comforts to which my love of country outings actually made me completely indifferent, we suffered at her place from the presence of a scourge that was far more dismaying: there was nothing in her house that was not sticky or did not cling to our fingers, whenever we wanted to pick up a tool, or our elbows had the misfortune to bump into a piece of furniture; even our eyes, literally, could perceive the viscous film that covered every single thing. We never lunched or dined with her there and, only too happy to plead the necessity for picnics ("The weather is so fine, it would be a crime not to have lunch on the banks of the Golotte"), we would head off elsewhere with relief in our hearts.

The countryside. All my life I have lived in the city, intoxicated with the marble surfaces that pave the vestibule of my residence, or the red carpet that muffles one's steps and feelings, or the Delft glass that decorates the stairwell, or the luxurious woodwork that discreetly panels the precious boudoir we call an elevator. Every day, every week, when I returned from my meals in the provinces, I would find myself once again on the asphalt, and in the distinguished veneer of my bourgeois residence, locking up my hunger for greenery between four walls crammed full of masterpieces, and every time I would forget more definitively that I was born for trees. The countryside . . . My green cathedral . . . It was there that my heart has sung its most fervent hymns, that my eyes learned the secrets of looking, my taste buds the flavor of game and of the vegetable garden, and my nose the elegance of fragrances. For in spite of the repulsive aspect of her lair, aunt Marthe did possess a treasure. I have met the greatest specialists in everything that has to do, however remotely, with the world of taste. Those who claim to be cooks must resort to all five senses to be truly cooks. A dish must be a delight to the eyes, the nose, and the taste, of course—but also to the touch, which directs the chef's choice on so many occasions and has its part to play in the celebration of fine food. It is true that hearing would seem to have no part to play; but one does not eat in silence, or in the midst of a din; any sound which interferes with the tasting process may either contribute or disturb that process, in such a way that a meal is indisputably kinesthetic. Thus I was often called on to feast with specialists of smell who were lured by the aromas emanating from kitchens, after a time spent in pursuit of those which migrated from flowers.

Not one of them will ever have as fine a nose as aunt
Marthe. Because the old nag was a Nose, a true one, a
great one, a huge Nose who didn't know she was a nose,
but whose unprecedented sensitivity would never have
suffered from the competition, had there been any. Thus,
this coarse, almost illiterate woman, this piece of human
scum casting her rotten foul stench onto everyone around
her, had created a garden fragrant with paradise. Through
a knowing tangle of wildflowers, honeysuckle and old rose
whose faded hue had been carefully preserved, a vegetable
garden scattered with brilliant peonies and blue sage
proudly displayed the most beautiful lettuce leaves in the
region. Cascades of petunias, groves of lavender, a few
steadfast box trees, ancestral wisteria along the front wall
of the house: from this well-orchestrated jumble emanated
the best of her being, that neither dirt nor fetid exhalations
nor the sordid aspect of a life devoted to vacuousness
could manage to enshroud. How many old women in the
countryside are gifted in this way with an extraordinary
sensory intuition which they apply to their gardening, or to
making herbal potions, or to cooking rabbit stew with
thyme, old women who then die as unknown geniuses,
their gift ignored by all—for most often we fail to see that
something so seemingly trivial and inconsequential, a
chaotic garden deep in the countryside, can belong with
the most beautiful works of art. In this reverie of flowers
and vegetables, beneath my dust-brown feet I crushed the
dry thick grass of the garden, and grew drunk on its fragrances.

First of all, the geranium leaves: I would lie on my stomach among the tomatoes and peas and, swooning with
pleasure, rub the leaves between my fingers: slightly acid,

sufficiently tart with a vinegary insolence, but not so tart that they could fail to evoke at the same time the delicately bitter scent of candied lemon, with a hint of the acrid odor of tomato leaves, whose boldness and fruitiness they preserve—that is what geranium leaves exhale, that is what I was growing drunk on, with my belly to the ground in the vegetable garden and my head in the flowers, ferreting for fragrance with all the concupiscence of the famished. Oh, magnificent memories of a time when I was the sovereign of a realm without artifice . . . In whole battalions, legions of red, white, yellow, and pink carnations stood proudly in the four corners of the courtyard, swelling their ranks each year with new recruits to become an army of serried troops and, through some inexplicable miracle, they did not slump from the weight of their overgrown stems, but bravely lifted their odd, chiseled corollas, incongruous in such tight configuration, scowling, but wafting all around a powdery fragrance, like that of beauties on their way to the ball . . .

Above all there was the linden tree. Immense and decorative, from one year to the next it threatened to submerge the house with its tentacular foliage, which my aunt obstinately refused to prune; any discussion was out of the question. During the hottest days of summer, the tree's troublesome shade offered the most sweet-smelling of bowers. I would sit against the trunk on the little bench of worm-eaten wood and avidly inhale the scent of pure, velvety honey which came from the tree's pale yellow flowers. A linden tree releasing its perfume at the end of the day is a rapture which leaves an indelible mark, and in the depths of our joy to be alive it traces a groove of happiness that the sweetness of a July evening alone cannot suffice to explain. Filling my lungs with that scent, in memory, which has not neared my nostrils in many a year, I have finally understood what it was that gave it its aroma: the complicity of honey and that very particular smell of the tree's leaves after a long spell of hot weather, where they are saturated with the dust of the fine summer days, and this evokes the absurd yet sublime feeling of imbibing from the air a concentrated essence of summer. Oh those fine summer days! When your body is free of the constraints of winter, when at last you can feel the caress of a breeze against your naked skin, offered to the world, blatantly open to it, in an ecstasy of freedom regained . . . In the motionless air, saturated with the buzzing of invisible insects, time stands still . . . The poplar trees along the tow-paths sing to the breezes a melody of verdant rustling, between light and shimmering shadow . . . A cathedral, yes, a cathedral of light-splattered greenery encircled me with its immediate, clear beauty . . . Even the jasmine at nightfall in the streets of Rabat never attained such evocative power . . . I am following the thread of a scent belonging to the linden . . . Languorous swaying of branches, a bee gathering pollen at the edge of my vision . . . I remember . . .

She had picked it, that particular one among all the others, she had not hesitated for an instant. I have since learned that this is what makes for excellence, this impression of ease and certainty in an instance where we know that it actually takes centuries of experience, a will of iron and the discipline of a monk. Where did Aunt Marthe derive her science from—a science made up of hydrometry, solar radiation, biological maturation, photosynthesis,

geodesic orientations and many other factors that my igno-
rance will not venture to enumerate? For what an ordinary
human might know from experience and reflection, she
knew instinctively. Her acute discernment swept over the
surface of the vegetable garden and measured its climate in
a microsecond that no ordinary perception of time could
detect—and she knew. She knew as surely and with the
same nonchalance as if I had said, The weather is fine, she
knew which of these little red globes had to be picked
now. In her dirty hand, deformed by work in the fields,
there it sat: crimson in its taut silken finery, undulating
with the occasional more tender hollow, with a communi-
cable cheerfulness about it like a plumpish woman in her
party dress hoping to compensate for the inconvenience of
her extra pounds by means of a disarming chubbiness
evoking an irresistible desire to bite into her flesh.
Sprawled on the bench beneath the linden tree, lulled by
the low murmuring of the leaves, I woke from a voluptuous nap, and beneath this canopy of sugary honey I bit
into the fruit, I bit into the tomato.

In salads, baked, in ratatouille, in preserves, grilled,
stuffed, cherry, candied, big and soft, green and acidic,
honored with olive oil or coarse salt or wine or sugar or
hot pepper, crushed, peeled, in a sauce, in a stew, in a
foam, even in a sorbet: I thought I had thoroughly covered
the matter and on more than one occasion I wrote pieces
inspired by the greatest chefs' menus claiming that I had
penetrated its secret. What an idiot, what a pity . . . I
invented mysteries where there were none, in order to justify my perfectly pathetic métier. What is writing, no matter how lavish the pieces, if it says nothing of the truth,
cares little for the heart, and is merely subservient to the

pleasure of showing one's brilliance? And yet I had always been acquainted with the tomato, since the time of Aunt Marthe's garden, since the summer when an ever more ardent sun kissed the timid little growths, since the moment my teeth tore into the flesh to splatter my tongue with the rich, warm and bountiful juice, whose essential generosity is masked by the chill of a refrigerator, or the affront of vinegar, or the false nobility of oil. Sugar, water, fruit, pulp, liquid or solid? The raw tomato, devoured in the garden when freshly picked, is a horn of abundance of simple sensations, a radiating rush in one's mouth that brings with it every pleasure. The resistance of the skin— slightly taut, just enough; the luscious yield of the tissues, their seed-filled liqueur oozing to the corners of one's lips, and that one wipes away without any fear of staining one's fingers; this plump little globe unleashing a flood of nature inside us: a tomato, an adventure.

Beneath the hundred-year-old linden, between perfume and palate, I would bite into the plump purple globes that Aunt Marthe had brought me with the vague sensation that I was in the presence of a capital truth. A capital truth—but one which, still, is not the one I seek now at the gates of death. It has been decreed that on this morning I shall drink my despair to the dregs, for I have strayed from the place to which my heart is calling. The raw tomato, no, that is not yet what I have been searching for . . . and now another raw delight has entered my thoughts.

(Violette)

Ruc de Grenelle, the Kitchen

Poor Madame. To see her like this, a real suffering soul, she just doesn't know what to do anymorc. It's truc he's really in a bad way . . . I didn't recognize him! How you can change in a day, I'd no idea. Violette, said Madame, some food he's after, you understand, something he's after but he doesn't know what. At first I didn't understand. Some food he's after, Madame, well does he want it or not? He's searching, searching, something that would make him feel good, she answered, but he can't find it. And she was wringing her hands, what is he thinking, to get all worked up over some dish when you're about to die; if I were going to die tomorrow, you can be sure I wouldn't be bothered about eating!

I do everything here. Well, almost everything. When I first started here thirty years ago, it was as a cleaning lady. Madame and Monsieur had only just gotten married, they had some property, I think, but not a whole lot, all the same. Just enough to hire a cleaning lady three times a week. The money came later, lots of money, I could see it was happening very quickly and that they expected there would be more and more money, because they moved into this big apartment, the same one we're in today, and Madame started doing a lot of work on the place, she was very cheerful, she was happy, you could tell, and she was so pretty! So once Monsieur was firmly established in his career they hired other servants and Madame kept me on as a "housekeeper," with better pay, full time, to "supervise" the others: the cleaning woman, the butler, the gardener (there's only a large terrace, but the gardener always finds things to do, in fact he's my husband, so there will always be a job for him). Mind now, don't go thinking this isn't work, I run around all day, I have my inventories to draw up, lists, orders to give, and while I don't want to act all important, if I weren't here, frankly, nothing would run smoothly in this house.

I do like Monsieur. I know he's got his faults, and one of them is that he's made poor Madame so unhappy, not just today but right from the start, always off somewhere, always coming back and never asking for any news, looking at her as if she were transparent and giving her presents the way you give someone a tip. Not to mention the children. I wonder if Laura will come. I used to think, before, that when he got old everything would work out, that he'd end up being more gentle, and then grandchildren are supposed to reconcile parents with their children, you can't resist. Of course, Laura doesn't have any children. But still. You'd think she'd come . . .

I like Monsieur for two reasons. First, because he has always been polite and kind with me, and with Bernard my husband as well. More polite and kind than with his wife and kids. That's the way he is, well-mannered enough to say, "Good morning, Violette, how are you today? Is your son feeling better?" but he hasn't said good morning to his wife for twenty years. The worst of it is that he seems sincere, with his big, loud, kindly voice, he's not proud, no, not at all, he's always very courteous with us. And he looks at me, and he pays attention to what I say to him, and he smiles because I'm always in a good mood, always busy doing something, I never rest and I know he's listening to my answers because he answers me too when I question him in return: "And you, Sir, how are you this morning?" "Fine, fine, Violette, but I'm behind with my work and it's not getting any better, I've got to get going," and he winks at me before he disappears down the corridor. Now, he wouldn't be like that with his wife. He likes people like us, Monsieur does, he prefers us, you can tell. I think he feels more at ease with us than with all those upper crust sorts he hangs around with: you can tell he's glad he can please them and impress them, stuff them full of food and watch them listening to him, but he doesn't like them; it's not his world.

The second reason I like Monsieur, it's kind of hard to put in words . . . it's because he farts in bed! The first time I heard it, I couldn't figure out what it was I'd heard, so to speak . . . And then it happened again, it was seven in the morning, it came from the corridor to the little salon where Monsieur sometimes slept when he came home late at night, a sort of detonation, a false note, but I mean really loud; I'd never heard anything like it! And then I understood, and I couldn't stop laughing, I laughed till I cried. I was bent over double, I had a bellyache, but at least I had the presence of mind to go to the kitchen, I sat down on a bench, I thought I'd never catch my breath! From that day on I've felt particularly well-disposed toward Monsieur, yes, well-disposed, because my husband farts in bed, too (but not as loud, all the same). A man who farts in bed, my grandmother used to say, is a man who loves life. And then, too, I don't know: it made me feel closer to him . . .

I know exactly what it is that Monsieur wants. It's not a dish, it's not something to eat. It's the lovely blonde lady who came here twenty years ago with a sad look on her face, a very gentle lady, very elegant, and she asked me, "Is Monsieur at home?" And I answered, "No, but Madame is here." She raised an eyebrow, I could tell she was surprised, and then she turned on her heel and I never saw her again, but I'm sure there was something between them and that if he didn't love his wife it was because he was missing the tall blonde lady in the fur coat.

Raw

Rue de Grenelle, the Bedroom

To return is to discover perfection. That is why only decadent civilizations are susceptible to the return: it is in Japan, where refinement has attained unequalled heights, at the heart of a millennial culture that has given humanity its greatest contributions, that the return to raw food, in its latest manifestation, has been possible. It is at the heart of old Europe—like my own self, endlessly dying—that for the first time since prehistory people have been eating raw meat seasoned with a mere sprinkling of spices.

Raw food. One would be wrong to believe that this involves nothing more than the coarse consumption of unprepared matter! Slicing into raw fish is like cutting into stone. To a novice a block of marble seems monolithic. If you try to place your chisel at random and strike a blow, the tool will jump out of your hands, while the stone will preserve its integrity, unaffected. A good marble worker knows his material. He senses where the cut—which already exists, just waiting to be revealed—will yield to his blow, and he has already divined, to the nearest millimeter, the figure that will be drawn forth, a figure which only the uninformed might impute to the will of the sculptor. No, on the contrary, the sculptor merely unveils the shape—for talent consists not in inventing shapes but in causing those that were invisible to emerge.

The Japanese chefs of my acquaintance only became masters in the art of raw fish after years of apprenticeship, where the cartography of flesh was gradually brought to light. It is true that some people already have the gift, can feel beneath their fingers the fault lines along which the offered creature shall be transformed into delectable sashimi, of the sort only experts know how to exhume from the tasteless entrails of the fish. But they do not become artists for all that until they have mastered their innate talent, and learned that instinct alone cannot suffice: they will also need agility in slicing, discernment in determining what is best, and strength of character to reject anything that is mediocre. The chef Tsuno, the greatest of them all, was known to take from a gigantic salmon only a single tiny piece that seemed a paltry amount. In this matter, in fact, abundance is meaningless: perfection orders everything. A tiny fragment of fresh flesh, on its own, naked, raw: perfect.

I knew him when he was already advanced in years, when he had deserted his own kitchen and would observe the customers from behind the bar, without ever touching a plate. Once in a great while, however, in honor of a guest or a particular occasion, he would return to his work—but only for sashimi. In his latter years these already exceptional occasions became increasingly rare, until they came to be considered extraordinary events.

I was a young critic at the time, whose career was still a matter of promising beginnings, and I still concealed the arrogance that only later would be recognized as the mark of my genius, but which, at the time, would have come across as mere pretension. It was therefore with feigned humility that I went to sit at the Kamogawa sushi bar, alone, for a dinner that I expected to be honorable. I had never tasted any raw fish in my life, and hoped to discover a new source of pleasure. Nothing in my budding career in gastronomy had in fact prepared me for such a thing. The only word that mattered to me at the time was *terroir*—but today I know that a *terroir* only exists by virtue of one's childhood mythology , and that if we have invented these worlds of tradition rooted deep in the land and identity of a region, it is because we want to solidify and objectify the magical, bygone years that preceded the horror of becoming an adult. Only a fanatical will to make a vanished world endure despite the passing of time can explain this belief in the existence of a *terroir*—an entire world that has disappeared, a mixture of flavors, smells, scattered fragrances that has left its sediment in ancestral rites and local dishes, crucibles of illusory memories that seek to make gold from sand, eternity from time. There is no great cuisine, without evolution, without erosion and forgetting. Invention must constantly be invoked upon the countertop, and past and future, here and elsewhere, raw and cooked, savory and sweet shall all be mixed, for it is this inventiveness that has made cuisine into an art that thrives untrammeled by the obsession of those who do not wish to die.

It is no exaggeration therefore to say that between cassoulets and cabbage stew I arrived at the Kamogawa sushi bar completely innocent of any contact—but not of preconceived ideas—with Japanese cuisine. Hidden by a host of cooks, at the back to the right, was a little man slumped in a chair. The restaurant was bare, the room Spartan, the chairs basic, but a cheerful hubbub reigned, the sort you hear in places where guests are satisfied with the food and with the service. Nothing surprising. Nothing special. Why did he do it? Did he know who I was, had word of my budding reputation in the little gastronomy fraternity spread to the ears of this blasé old man? Was it for his sake? Was it for mine? What causes a mature man, who has outlived all his emotions, to revive a faltering internal flame after all, and for one last show set his vital force ablaze? What is at stake in the confrontation between a man who is abdicating and one who is conquering—is it lineage, is it renunciation? It remains a fathomless mystery: not once did he turn his gaze on me, except at the end— his eyes empty, ravaged, signifying nothing.

When he got up off of his rickety chair, a stony silence gradually fell over the restaurant. First of all upon the cooks, who were petrified with stupor, and then, it was as if an invisible wave suddenly broke over all those present, upon the customers at the bar, then those in the room, until the silence reached those who had just come in and who stood watching the scene, dumbfounded. He had gotten up without saying a word and walked over to the counter, opposite me. The man whom earlier I had assumed was leading the team bowed briefly, a gesture filled with the absolute respect so characteristic of Asian cultures, and then he slowly stepped back, with all the others, toward the gaping kitchens, although they did not go in, but just stood there, motionless, devout. Chef Tsuno elaborated upon his composition there before me with gentle, sparing gestures, displaying an economy of movement that bordered on indigence, but I could see beneath his palm the birth and blossoming, in mother of pearl and

moiré, of slivers of flesh, pink and white and gray; fascinated, I sat watching the miracle.

It was dazzling. What would then pass through the barrier of my teeth was neither matter nor water, merely an
intermediary substance that had retained of the former the
texture and consistency that prevent it from evaporating
into nothingness, and had borrowed from the latter the
miraculous fluidity and smoothness. True sashimi is not so
much bitten into as allowed to melt on the tongue. It calls
for slow, supple chewing, not to bring about a change in
the nature of the food but merely to allow one to savor its
airy, satiny texture. Yes, it is like a fabric: sashimi is velvet
dust, verging on silk, or a bit of both, and the extraordinary alchemy of its gossamer essence allows it to preserve
a milky density unknown even by clouds. The first pink
mouthful to evoke such a thrill was salmon, but I had yet
to try plaice, scallops, and octopus. Salmon is oily and
sweet, despite its essential leanness; octopus is pure and
rigorous, loath to divulge its secret liaisons to one's bite,
and then only after a long resistance. I would stare at the
strange, lacy little piece of flesh before siezing upon it, all
marbled pink and purple but almost black at the tip of its
crenellated excrescences; I would clumsily pick it up with
my chopsticks, which only complied with difficulty, and
place it upon my tongue—which contracted at such novel
d e n s i t y—and I would shiver with pleasure. Between the
two, between the salmon and the octopus, came the entire
palette of sensations, each characterized by the same compact fluidity which places heaven on one's tongue and
makes any additional liquid, whether it is water, Kirin, or
warm sake, utterly superfluous. As for the scallop, it was

so light and evanescent that it slipped away the moment it arrived, but long afterward, my cheeks recalled the effects of its profound caress. Last of all came the plaice, which, mistakenly, seemed to be the most rustic of all, for it is a lemony delicacy, and its exceptional constitution is confirmed the moment one bites into it and discovers its stupefying plenitude.

That is sashimi: a fragment of the cosmos within reach of one's heart, but, alas, light years from the fragrance or taste that is fleeing my wisdom, or is it my inhumanity . . . I thought that by evoking this subtle adventure into the territory of raw delights, a thousand leagues from the barbarity of those who devour animals, something might give off the perfume of authenticity that is inspiring that unknown memory, the memory I despair of ever capturing . . . Shellfish, yet again, it must be shellfish: yet perhaps it's simply not the right one?

(Chabrot)

Rue de Bourgogne, Medical Offices

Three possible paths.

The asymptotic path: a wretched salary, green scrubs, long shifts as an intern, a probable career, the path of power, the path of honors. Professor of Cardiology. The public hospital, devotion to the cause, love of science: just the right amount of ambition, nous, and skill. I was ripe for all that.

The middle path: everyday life. Lots and lots of money. A posh clientele, teeming with depressive bourgeois ladies, rich and extravagant old men, sun-tanned drug addicts, angina, flu, and long and immeasurable ennui. The Montblanc my wife offers me every twenty-fifth of December slides over the whiteness of the prescription pad. I raise my head, crack a smile at the right moment, a bit of comfort here, a bit of politeness there, a lot of false humanity everywhere and for a price I am able to grant to Madame Derville, the wife of the president of the Bar, absolution from the anxieties caused by her condition as an incurable hysteric.

The tangential path: treat souls not bodies. Journalist, writer, painter, *éminence grise*, a mandarin of letters, archeologist? Anything at all, save the panels of my worldly doctor's office, save the famous and well-paid anonymity of my curative charge, in my affluent neighborhood, in my minister's armchair . . .

The middle path, naturally. And stretching ahead, decades of nagging dissatisfaction, inner turmoil, sometimes eating away at me, sometimes virulent, sometimes hidden—but always present.

The first time he consulted me, I caught a glimpse of my salvation. He made a gift to me of the very thing that I—too corrupted by my bourgeois blood to renounce it—could not be, merely by tacitly agreeing to be my client, simply by frequenting my waiting room on a regular basis, with his ordinary docile manner of a patient who makes no fuss. Later he gave me another gift, magnanimously: that of his conversation. Worlds hitherto unknown to me suddenly appeared, and the very thing that my flame had always coveted so ardently, and had despaired of ever obtaining, was suddenly mine, thanks to him, vicariously.

To live vicariously: to give birth to one chef and be another's gravedigger, to extract words from a feast, phrases, symphonies of language, and to give birth to the dazzling beauty inherent in a meal; to be a Maître, a Guide, a Divinity; to touch inaccessible spheres with one's mind, to penetrate stealthily into the labyrinths of inspiration, come close to perfection, and touch on Genius! What should one's preference be, truly? To live one's sorry little life as a good obedient Homo sapiens, without purpose, without salt, because one is too weak to stick to one's objective? Or, almost trespassing, to share endlessly in the ecstasy of another who knows his quest, who has already begun his crusade and who, because he has an ultimate goal, partakes of immortality?

Later still, there were other exemplars of his largesse: his friendship. By accepting the gaze he bestowed upon me, in the privacy of our man-to-man conversations where I became, in the heat of my passion for Art, the witness, the disciple, the protector and admirer all at the same time, I received a hundredfold the fruit of my willing subordination. His friendship! Who has not dreamt of friendship with a Great Man in our century, who has not longed to walk shoulder to shoulder with the Hero, to confer accolades on the prodigal son, the great Maître of those who love to gorge themselves on fine fare? His friend! His friend and confidant, granted the ultimate privilege, oh how precious and painful at the same time, to have to bring him the news of his own death . . . Is it for tomorrow? At dawn? Or during the night? The night . . . It is my night too, because the witness dies when he can no longer testify, because the disciple dies in the agony of loss, because the protector dies when he has failed, and the admirer, finally, dies from adoring a corpse doomed to the tranquility of the graveyard . . . My night . . .

But I regret nothing, and ask for everything: because it was he, because it was myself.

The Mirror

Rue de Grenelle, the Bedroom

His name was Jacques Destrères. It was at the very beginning of my career. I had just completed an article on the specialty of the Gerson restaurant, the very article that would revolutionize the accepted structure of my profession and place me in the firmament of food criticism. I awaited with excitement yet confidence for what was to follow, and had taken refuge with my uncle, my father's older brother, an old bachelor who knew how to live and whom everyone in my family regarded as an eccentric. He had never married, nor had we ever even seen a woman by his side, and my father suspected him of being "one of them." He had done well in business and in his old age had retired to a lovely little property near the Rambouillet forest, where he spent tranquil days pruning his rose bushes, walking his dogs, smoking a cigar in the company of a few old business relations and concocting his little bachelor's meals.

Sitting in his kitchen, I watched him at work. It was wintertime. I had had an early lunch Chez Groers, in Versailles, and then made my way along the snowy little back roads in what was an exceedingly good mood. The fire was burning merrily in the hearth, and my uncle was fixing us a meal. The kitchen at my grandmother's had accustomed me to a noisy, feverish atmosphere where, amidst the clanging of saucepans, the sizzling of butter and the chop-chop of knives toiled a virago in a trance, and only her long experience granted her an aura of serenity—of the sort displayed by martyrs in the flames of hell. Jacques, on the other hand, undertook everything with moderation. He did not hurry, nor was he slow. Every gesture came in its own good time.

He rinsed the jasmine rice in a silvery little colander, drained it, poured it into a saucepan, covered it with one and a half times its volume in salted water, put a lid on the pan, and let it cook. The shrimp waited in an earthenware bowl. While he was chatting with me, mostly about my article and my projects, he was shelling the shrimp with painstaking concentration. Not for one moment did he step up the pace, not for one moment did he slow down. When the last little arabesque had been stripped of its protective shell, he conscientiously washed his hands with a soap that smelled of milk. With the same serene uniformity in his gestures, he placed a cast iron frying pan on the stove, poured a trickle of olive oil into it, let it heat, then scattered the peeled shrimp into the pan. His wooden spatula adroitly circled the shellfish, not allowing a single tiny crescent to escape, scooping them from every side and causing them to dance on the fragrant grill. Then some curry. Neither too much nor too little. A sensual dust tinged the pinky copper of the crustaceans with an exotic gold: the Orient, rein-vented. Salt, pepper. With his scissors he snipped a branch of cilantro above the frying pan. Finally, very quickly, a cap-ful of cognac, a match; a long, angry flame leapt up from the pan, like a shout or a cry set free at last, a raging sigh fading as quickly as it flared.

Waiting patiently on the marble table were a porcelain plate, a crystal glass, superb cutlery and an embroidered linen napkin. On the plate he carefully arranged, with the wooden spoon, half of the shrimp, and the rice, which had been placed in a tiny bowl then turned upside down to create a plump little dome, crowned with a mint leaf. Into the glass he poured a generous helping of a transparent wheat-colored liquid.

"Shall I pour you a glass of Sancerre?"

I shook my head. He sat down at the table.

A bite to eat. This is what Jacques Destrères called a bite to eat. And I knew he wasn't joking, that every day he would take great pains to cook himself a little mouthful of paradise, unaware of how refined his everyday fare was, a true gourmet; he lived every day as an authentic aesthete, where absolutely nothing was staged. Without touching the food he had prepared before my eyes, I watched him eat with the same detached, subtle care that he had put into cooking his meal, and this meal that I did not touch remained one of the most delicious I have ever tasted in my life.

Tasting is an act of pleasure, and writing about that pleasure is an artistic gesture, but the only true work of art, in the end, is another person's feast. Jacques Destrères's meal had all the perfection of a feast because it was not my feast, because it did not spill over onto the before and after of my everyday life, and it could remain in my memory as a closed and self-sufficient unity, a unique moment etched there outside of time and space, a pearl of my spirit released from the feelings in my life. As if one were looking into a room reflected in a sunburst mirror, which turns into a painting because it is no longer opened onto something else, but merely suggests an entire world without an elsewhere, strictly confined within the edges of the mirror and isolated from any life around it: another person's meal is enclosed within the frame of our gaze, and is exempt from the infinite vanishing line of our own memories or projects. I would have liked to live that life, the one evoked by the mirror, or by Jacques's plate, a life without prospects, for the possibility of that life becoming a work of art would vanish through the mirror, would be a life with neither once upon a time, nor ever after, with neither surroundings nor horizons: just the here and now—beautiful, full, enclosed.

But that is not it. Everything that the fine restaurants brought to my nourishing genius, everything that Destrères's shrimp might have suggested to my intelligence cannot teach my heart a thing. Spleen. Black sun. The sun . . .

(Gégène)

Corner of the rue de Grenelle
and the rue du Bac

Y ou and I are made of the same cloth.
There are two categories of passersby. First of all,
the most common category, even though it does
contain some nuances: these are the people who won't
ever meet my gaze, or if they do, it is just fleetingly, when
they give me some change. There's a faint smile there too,
sometimes, but always as if they were a little embarrassed,
and then they hurry away fast as they can. Or they don't
stop at all and go by as quickly as possible, with their guilty
conscience bugging them for a hundred meters or so—
fifty before, when they've seen me from a distance and
make haste to screw their head in the other direction, until
they're safely fifty meters past the ragamuffin, when their
head can regain its customary mobility—then they can forget me, they can breathe easy again, and that wrenching
moment of pity and shame gradually fades away. I know
what those people say when they go home at night, if they
even think about it again, in some place deep in their
unconscious: "It's awful, there are more and more of them,
it breaks your heart, I give them something, of course I do,
but after the second one I have to draw the line, I know,
it's arbitrary, it's horrible, but you can't go on giving endlessly, when I think of all the taxes we pay, it shouldn't be
up to us to give, it's the State which is at fault, it's the State

which isn't doing its bit, and even so it's a good job we've got a left-wing government, otherwise it would be even worse. Right? What's for dinner tonight, pasta?"

I'd fuck them dry, I would. And that's being polite. To hell with them, those pinky bourgeois, they want their cake and they want to eat it too, they want their season ticket to the Châtelet and want to see the down-and-outs rescued from poverty, they want their tea at Mariage's and all men on earth to be equal, they want their vacation in Tuscany and to see the sidewalks swept clean of anything that might stimulate their guilt, they want to pay their cleaning lady off the books and they want you to listen to their altruistic I'm-a-defender-of-humanity tirades. The State, the State! They're like illiterate folk who adore the king and accuse only the evil corrupt ministers of all the ills they're subject to; it's the Godfather saying to his minions, "I don't like the look of this guy," without acknowledging that what he has just ordered in a veiled sort of way is the man's execution; it's the bullied sons or daughters who insult the social worker asking for explanations from unworthy parents! The State! It's only fair to go after the State when you want to blame someone else, even if that someone else is none other than your own self!

And then there's the other category. The brutes, the real bastards, the ones who don't hurry by, don't look away, they look right at me with their cold gaze, not a drop of compassion; tough luck, you old bum, you can just snuff it if you didn't know how to make it, no indulgence for the riffraff or the plebes vegetating in their subhuman cardboard boxes, we'll give them no quarter, it's win or lose, and if you think I'm ashamed of my money, well you're mistaken.

For ten years, day after day, he would set out from his palace and deliberately walk right by me with his smug rich man's step, and he'd stare down my plea with a calm and scornful gaze.

If I were him, I'd do the same. People shouldn't think that all tramps are lefties and that poverty makes you a revolutionary. And since word has it he's going to die, I say to him, "Go ahead and die, mate, die from all the money you never gave me, die from all your rich-bastard banquets, die from your life of power, but I sure won't be throwing up a cheer. We're made of the same cloth, you and I."

Bread

Rue de Grenelle, the Bedroom

We were breathless; it was time to leave the beach. The day had already seemed both deliciously short and long. The shoreline at this point, a long sandy arc stretching lazily into the distance and devoured by waves, offered us the most heedless of swims, with the maximum of pleasure and the minimum risk. Since morning, with my cousins, we had been diving over and over into the breakers, or taking flight from their crests, breathless, inebriated from the endless rollers, only returning to the common assembly point—the family parasol—just long enough to gobble a fritter or a bunch of grapes before racing hell for leather back into the ocean. There were times, however, when I would drop flat onto the hot, crunching sand and find myself instantly transfixed by a daze of well-being, only barely conscious of the drowsiness in my body and the customary sounds of the beach—from the cry of gulls to the laughter of children—an interlude of intimacy in the very singular stupor of happiness. But most of the time I drifted with the waves, surfacing and disappearing beneath their liquid, moving mass. Childhood exaltation: how many years do we spend forgetting the passion we breathed into any activity that held a promise of pleasure? Why are we now so rarely capable of such total commitment, such elation, such

flights of charming lyricism? There was so much exultation about those days spent swimming, so much simplicity . . . so soon replaced, alas, by the ever increasing difficulty of finding pleasure in things . . .

At around one in the afternoon we would strike camp.
On our way back to Rabat, a dozen or so kilometers away,
in the furnace of the car I had the leisure to admire the
waterfront. I never tired of it. Later, as a young man who
no longer partook of those Moroccan summers, I would
occasionally conjure up the most infinite details of the
road leading from the beach at Sables d'Or to the town,
and in town I would go back over the streets and gardens
with painstaking euphoria. It was a lovely road that over-
looked the Atlantic in many spots; villas submerged in ole-
ander offered glimpses through the false transparency of
wrought iron onto the sunny life being lived behind those
gates; farther along was the ochre fortress overlooking the
emerald water, and only much later would I learn that it
was nothing more than an ugly prison; then there was the
little beach of Temara, sheltered, protected from wind and
current, and I eyed it scornfully with the disdain of those
who only appreciate the sea for its harshness and turbulence; the next beach along, too dangerous for swimming,
was scattered with a few intrepid fishermen, their brown
legs whipped by waves as if the ocean wanted to swallow
them in a raging roar; then came the outskirts of the city,
the souk teeming with sheep and the light-colored canvas
of awnings snapping in the wind, the neighborhoods
swarming with joyful, noisy neighborhoods swarming
with people, poor but healthy in the salt air. The sand
clung to my ankles, my cheeks were burning, I grew
drowsy with the heat in the car and let myself be lulled by

the melodic yet forceful tones of Arabic, rocked to the rhythm of incomprehensible snatches of conversation stolen through the open window. A sweet ordeal, the sweetest of all: those who have spent their summers by the seaside know what this means, the exasperating necessity of *heading back*, of leaving the water for the land, of enduring the discomfort of becoming heavy and sweaty once again; they will know what it means, they have cursed it, but remember it, on other occasions, as a blessed moment. The holiday rituals, immutable sensations: the taste of salt at the corner of one's lips, shriveled fingertips, hot, dry skin, sticky hair still dripping slightly down one's neck, shortness of breath, what a pleasure it was, how easy it was . . . Once we arrived home we would make a dash for the shower and re-emerge gleaming, our skin soft, our hair tamed, and the afternoon would begin with a meal.

We would buy it carefully wrapped in newspaper, at a little shop outside the city walls before we climbed back into the car. I would look at it out of the corner of my eye; I was still too dazed to make the most of its presence, but I was reassured to know it was there, for "afterwards," for lunch. Strange . . . That this most visceral memory of bread, coming to me on this day of death, is that of a Moroccan *kesra*, a lovely, flat round, closer to a cake in consistency than to a baguette, does not fail to leave me pondering. Whatever the case may be, once I was rinsed off and dressed, blissfully awaiting my post-beach stroll through the medina, I would sit down at the table, tear off a first conquering mouthful from the sizeable chunk that my mother handed me, and in the yielding, golden warmth of this food I found once again the consistency of sand, its color and welcoming presence. Bread, beach: two related sources of warmth, two alluring accomplices; every time, an entire world of rustic joy invades our perception. It's a fallacy to claim that what accounts for the nobility of bread is the way it suffices unto itself while accompanying all other dishes. If bread "suffices unto itself," it is because it is multiple, not because it exists in multiple variants but in its very essence: bread is rich, bread is diverse, bread is a microcosm. Bread contains such stunning diversity; it is akin to a miniature world which reveals its inner workings as it is consumed. You storm it through an initial encounter with the barrier of crust, then yield to wonder the moment you are through, as the fresh soft interior consents. There is such a divide between the crunchy shell— on occasion as hard as stone, at other times mere show, quickly yielding to the charge, and the tenderness of the inner substance which lodges in one's cheeks with a docile charm—that one is almost at a loss. The fissures in the envelope are like unexpected rural missives: one thinks of a ploughed field, of a peasant in the evening air; the village steeple has just rung seven o'clock; the peasant is wiping his forehead with the lapel of his jacket; his labors done.

Where the crust meets the soft bread, on the other hand, our inner gaze encounters a mill; the dust from the wheat whirls around the millstone, the air is infested with a volatile powder; and the picture changes once again, because your palate has just taken possession of the honeycombed foam, now freed from its yoke, and the labor of the jaw can begin. It is indeed bread, and yet you can eat it like cake; but chewing bread, unlike pastry, or even sweet breakfast rolls, leads to a surprising result, to a . . .

sticky result. As you chew and chew upon the soft interior, a sticky mass is formed, which no air can penetrate: the bread adheres—yes, like glue. If you have never dared to take a mass of soft dough between your teeth and tongue and palate and cheeks, you have never thrilled to the feeling of jubilant ardor that viscosity can convey. It is no longer bread, nor dough, nor cake that we are masticating; it is something like our own self, what our own secret tissues must taste like, as we knead them with our expert mouths, saliva and yeast mingling in ambiguous fraternity.

Around the table, we ruminated in silence, conscientiously. There do exist some strange communions, after all . . . We were far from the rituals and banquets of institutional ceremonies—it was not a religious act of breaking bread and rendering grace to Heaven, yet we were nevertheless united in a holy communion that caused us to attain, unbeknownst to us, a higher, all-decisive truth. And while a few of us might have been vaguely aware of this mystical orison, misguidedly attributing it to the pleasure of being together, of sharing a consecrated delicacy, within the convivial and relaxed atmosphere of summer holidays, I knew that their misapprehension arose for lack of the words and knowledge with which to express and illuminate such an exalted moment. The rural countryside, far from town; the gentle way of life and organic elasticity: there is all that in bread, whether the bread is from here or elsewhere. That is what, without the shadow of a doubt, makes bread the preferred vehicle for inner contemplation, for drifting in search of ourselves.

After this initial appetizing contact, I would prepare for the next round of hostilities. Fresh salad—no need to point out the degree to which carrots and potatoes cut into tiny regular dice and seasoned with a hint of coriander are an improvement upon their more coarsely chopped fellows; then a bounty of tagines, causing me to lick my chops and stuff my face like an angel, without remorse or regret. But my mouth had not forgotten, my mouth remembered that this festive meal had been inaugurated by the encounter between its mandibles and a tender doughy mouthful, and even though to prove my gratitude I would go on to swoop the morsel into my plate to mop up all the sauce, I knew my heart was no longer in it. With bread, as with everything, it is the first time that counts.

I recall the flowery luxuriance of the Oudaia tea room, whence we could look out onto Salé and the sea, in the distance, just below the river which flowed beneath the city walls; the colorful narrow streets of the medina; the jasmine cascading down the walls of the inner courtyards, a poor man's wealth a thousand leagues from the luxury of perfumers in the West; life under the sun, in the end, which is not the same as life elsewhere, because living outdoors one views space differently . . . and the bread, round and flat, a dazzling aubade to the union of the flesh. I can tell . . . I can tell that I am close. There is something of all this in the thing I am searching for. There is something . . . but that's not quite it . . . bread . . . bread . . . But what else could it be? What else on earth do men live by, if not bread?

(Lotte)

Rue Delbet

I always said, I don't want to go there, I like Granny but I don't like Grampy, he frightens me, he has big black eyes, and then he's never happy to see us, never happy at all. That's why it's weird today. Because for once I would like to go there, I'd like to see Granny, and then Rick, and Maman is the one who doesn't want to go, she says Granpy is sick and we're going to disturb him. Granpy sick? It can't be. Jean is sick, yes, he's very sick but that doesn't matter, I like to be with him, I like it in summer when we go to the pebbles together, he takes a pebble and then he looks at it and he invents a story, if it's a big fat one it's a man who's eaten too much, so now he can't walk anymore, he rolls, and rolls, or else it's a little flat one, he's been walked on and boom, flat as a pancake, and lots of other stories like that.

As for Granpy, he never told me any stories, never, he doesn't like stories, and he doesn't like children, and he doesn't like noise, I remember one day, at Rudegrenele I was playing nicely with Rick and then with Anaïs, Paul's sister's daughter, we were having a good laugh, and he turned and looked at us, a nasty look, a *really* nasty look, I felt like crying and hiding, I didn't feel like laughing anymore at all, and he said to Granny but he didn't even look at her, "This noise must stop." So Granny put on her sad expression, she didn't answer him, she came to talk to us and she said, "Come, children, let's go play out on the square, Granpy is tired." When we got back from the square Granpy had left and we didn't see him anymore, we had dinner with Granny and Maman, and Adèle, Paul's sister, and we had a really good time again but I could see that Granny was sad.

When I ask Maman questions she always answers, No, everything is fine, all that is grownups' business, I mustn't worry about all that and she loves me very very much. That I know. But I also know a lot of other things. I know that Granpy doesn't love Granny anymore, and that Granny doesn't love herself anymore, that Granny loves Jean more than Maman or Laura but Jean hates Granpy and Granpy thinks Jean's disgusting. I know that Granpy thinks my papa is an imbecile. I know that Papa is mad at Maman for being Granpy's daughter, but also because she wanted to have me, and he didn't want any children, or at least not yet: I also know that Papa loves me very much and maybe even that he's mad at Maman for loving me so much when he didn't want me at all, and I know Maman is mad at me a little sometimes because she wanted me when Papa didn't. Oh yes, I know all that. I know that they're all unhappy because nobody loves the right person the way they should and because they don't understand that it's really their own self that they're mad at.

People think that children don't know anything. It's enough to make you wonder if grownups were ever children once upon a time.

The Farm

Rue de Grenelle, the Bedroom

I eventually ended up at this spruce little farm on the Côte de Nacre after two hours of fruitless efforts to find a gastro inn that had just recently opened and which, I'd been told, was somewhere near Colleville and the American cemetery. I have always liked this part of Normandy. Not for its cider, or its apples, its cream or its *poulets flambés au calvados* but for its vast beaches, where the strand is laid bare by the low tide, and where I truly grasped the meaning of the expression "between heaven and earth." I took long walks along Omaha Beach, I was somewhat stunned by solitude and space, I watched the gulls and the dogs roaming in the sand, I raised my palm to shelter my eyes to study the horizon, which taught me nothing, and I felt content and trusting, reinvigorated by this silent escapade.

That morning, a fine summer morning, clear and cool, I had been wandering in search of my gastro inn with increasing bad humor, lost down unlikely sunken lanes, gleaning along the way only contradictory directions. I eventually set off down a little road that ended in a cul-de-sac in the yard of a Norman stone farmhouse with a porch crowned by an impressive wisteria, windows overwhelmed by red geraniums, and freshly painted white shutters. At the front of the house, in the shade of a linden tree, a table had been set and five people (four men and a woman) were finishing their lunch. They did not know the address of the place I was looking for. When I inquired, for lack of a better solution, whether there was somewhere not too far away where I could find something to eat, they sniffed with a hint of scorn. "Better off eating at home," said one of the men in a tone that was heavy with innuendo. The man I assumed to be the master of the house placed his hand on the roof of my car, leaned in toward me, and suggested without further ado that I share their luncheon with them. I accepted.

Sitting beneath the linden tree, which was so fragrant that I nearly lost my appetite, I listened to them conversing over their coffee and calvados while the farmer, a plump young woman with a winsome dimple on either side of the corners of her mouth, served me with a smile.

Four *fine de claire* oysters, cold and salty, with neither lemon nor seasoning. Swallowed slowly, blessed for the imperious chill with which they cloaked my palate. "Oh, this is all that is left, there was a gross, twelve dozen, but the men, when they come in from work, have an appetite." She laughed softly.

Four oysters, unembellished. A complete and uncompromising prelude, royal in unpolished modesty. A glass of dry white wine, chilled, with a fruity refinement—"it's a Saché, we have a cousin in Touraine who gives us a good price!"

This is just to work up an appetite. The men next to me are unbelievably garrulous, talking cars. Cars that run. Cars that don't. Then there are those that grumble, or rebel, or make a fuss, or backfire, or chug breathlessly, or have trouble up the hills, or skid in the turns, the ones that judder, or smoke, or hiccup, or cough, or nose up, or strike back. Memories of a particularly stubborn Simca 1100 are honored with a long tirade. A nasty cold-assed bitch of a car that wouldn't start even in the middle of summer. They all nod their head, indignantly.

Two thin slices of raw smoked ham, silky and supple along languid folds, some salted butter, a hunk of bread. An overdose of vigorous taste and smooth texture: improbable but delectable. Another glass of the same white wine, which will accompany me for the rest of the meal. An enticing, charming, beguiling prologue.

"Yes, the forest is full of it," is the reply to my polite question about game in the region. "In fact," says Serge (there are also Claude and Christian, the master of the house, but I can't recall the name of the other fellow), "it's often the cause of accidents."

A few green asparagus stems, plum and tender enough to make you swoon. "This will keep you going while the rest is reheating," says the young woman hastily, no doubt thinking that I am surprised to see such a meager main course. "No, no," I said, "it's magnificent." Exquisite tone, rural, almost bucolic. She blushes and hurries away with a laugh.

Next to me, the conversation continues in finer form than ever, about game animals unexpectedly crossing the road through the forest. There is talk of a certain Germain who, on a moonless night, ran over an adventurous wild boar and, thinking in the dark that it was dead, tossed it into his trunk ("Just think, what luck!"), set off on his way.

Meanwhile the beast gradually came to and started to kick about in the trunk ("What a confounded ruckus!") and then, by dint of so much thumping with its muzzle, dented the car and managed to escape into the night. They are laughing like children.

Leftovers (enough to feed a regiment) of fattened chicken. An overabundance of cream, chunks of bacon, a pinch of black pepper, potatoes which I suspect come from Noirmoutier—and not an ounce of fat.

The conversation has taken a detour, setting off down the sinuous winding road of local spirits. Good ones, not-so-good ones, and those that are frankly undrinkable; illicit liquors, ciders that are too fermented, with rotten apples that were poorly washed and poorly crushed and poorly picked; supermarket calvados that tastes like syrup, and then the true calvados, which scorches your throat but perfumes your palate. The liquor of a certain renowned Père Joseph sets everyone off with peals of laughter: a disinfectant, that much is for sure, but not a digestif!

"I'm so sorry," says the young woman, who does not speak with the same accent as her husband, "there's no more cheese, I have to go shopping this afternoon."

I learn that Thierry Coulard's dog, a fine creature renowned for its sobriety, forgot itself one day and began to lap up a small puddle beneath the barrel, and either it had a seizure or was poisoned, and fell down stiff as a board and only escaped the claws of death thanks to an exceptionally sturdy constitution. They are holding their sides with mirth, I have trouble catching my breath.

An apple tart, with thin, crisp flaky pastry, and wedges

of golden fruit insolently veiled beneath the discreet caramel sugar crystals. I finish the bottle. At five in the afternoon she serves me a coffee with calvados. The men get to their feet, slap me on the back and say they're going back to work, and that if I'm still there in the evening they'll be glad to see me. I hug them like brothers and promise to come back someday, with a good bottle.

It was there, beneath the centuries-old tree at the farm in Colleville, to the tune of pigs making a confounded ruckus (to the utmost delight of those who will tell the story one day), that I enjoyed one of my finest meals. The food was simple and delicious, but what I really devoured—to the point of relegating oysters, ham, asparagus and chicken to the rank of secondary accompaniments—was the truculence of my hosts' language: the syntax may have been brutally sloppy, but it was oh so warm in its juvenile authenticity. I feasted on their words, yes, the words flowing at that get-together of country brothers, the sort of words that, at times, delight one much more than the pleasures of the flesh. Words: repositories for singular realities which they then transform into moments in an anthology, magicians that change the face of reality by adorning it with the right to become memorable, to be placed in a library of memories. Life exists only by virtue of the osmosis of words and facts, where the former encase the latter in ceremonial dress. Thus, the words of my chance acquaintances, crowning the meal with an unprecedented grace, had almost formed the substance of my feast in spite of myself, and what I had enjoyed so merrily was the verb, not the meat.

I am roused from my reverie by a dull sound, one that cannot fool my ears. Through my half-closed lids I can see Anna slipping furtively by in the corridor. This ability my wife has to move forward without walking, without altering her progression with the usual interruption of steps, has always made me suspect that such aristocratic fluidity was created for my sake alone. Anna . . . If you knew how happy I have been to rediscover that labile afternoon, between eau-de-vie and forest, tossing my head back to gulp down the eternity of words! Perhaps those are the inner workings of my vocation, between what is said, and what is eaten . . . and the flavor, still, escapes me, dizzyingly . . . I am drawn by my thoughts toward my life in the provinces . . . a large house . . . long walks through the fields . . . the dog at my feet, joyful and innocent . . .

(Venus)

Rue de Grenelle, the Study

I am a primitive Venus, a small fertility goddess with a naked alabaster body: large, generous hips, a prominent belly and breasts falling to my rounded thighs, which lie one against the other in a somewhat comically shy attitude. A woman rather than a gazelle: everything in me invokes flesh, not contemplation. And yet, he looks at me, he never stops looking at me, the instant he lifts his eyes from his page, the instant he begins to meditate and sets his long dark gaze upon me without seeing me. Other times, however, he scrutinizes me thoughtfully, trying to penetrate my immobile sculpture's soul, I can tell he is a whisker away from establishing contact, from guessing, conversing, and then suddenly he gives up and I have the exasperating feeling that I have just attended the performance of a man who is looking at himself in a two-way mirror, never suspecting for a moment that from behind the mirror, someone is observing him. And sometimes his fingertips graze over me, he rubs the folds of my splendid womanhood, wanders with his palms over my featureless face, and upon my ivory surface I can feel his fluid, all untamed emotional maladjustment. When he sits down at his desk and pulls the cord of the big copper lamp, and a ray of warm light flows onto my shoulders, I am reborn each time from this demiurgical light, I reemerge from nowhere, and this is the way it is for him with the flesh and blood creatures who cross his path in life, they are absent from memory when he turns his back upon them and, when once again they enter the field of his perception, they offer him a presence he cannot grasp. He looks at them, too, without seeing them, apprehends them in a void, the way a blind man gropes before him, because he thinks he is grasping hold of something, when in fact he is merely stirring up evanescence, embracing the void. His watchful, intelligent eyes are separated from what they see by an invisible veil that hinders his judgment, renders opaque that which could, however, be so easily illuminated by his wit. And the veil is that of his rigidity, of the distraught autocrat, with his perpetual anxiety that the person opposite him might turn out to be something other than an object he can dismiss from his vision at leisure, that this person might not be a freedom that could recognize his own . . .

When he looks for me, without ever finding me, when at last he resigns himself to lowering his eyes or to grabbing hold of the cord in order to annihilate my existence, he is fleeing, fleeing, fleeing the unbearable. How he desires other people; how he fears them.

Die, old man. There is no peace and there is no place for you in this life.

The Dog

Rue de Grenelle, the Bedroom

In the early hours of our companionship, I was relentlessly fascinated by the indisputable elegance with which he would lower his hindquarters; firmly wedged between his rear paws, his tail sweeping the ground with the regularity of a metronome, his little hairless pink tummy folding softly beneath his downy chest, he would sit down vigorously and raise his moist hazelnut eyes to me, and often I thought I could see something else there besides mere appetite.

I had a dog. Or rather, a snout on paws. A little receptacle of anthropomorphic projections. A loyal companion. A tail that kept time with his emotions. An overexcited kangaroo at certain times of the day. A dog, as I said. When he first came to the house, his plump little folds of flesh could easily have inspired in me a sort of silly-making tenderness; but in the space of a few weeks the little round ball had become a slender little dog with a well-defined muzzle, clear, luminous eyes, an inquisitive nose, a powerful chest and well-muscled paws. He was a Dalmatian, and I'd baptized him Rhett, in honor of *Gone with the Wind*, my favorite film, because if I had been a woman, I would have been Scarlett—the one who survives in a world that is dying. His immaculate fur, with its meticulous sprinkling of black, was incredibly silky; as it happens, the Dalmatian is a very silky dog, both to look at and to touch. Not in an unctuous way, however: there was nothing complacent or sappy about the immediate sympathy that his physiognomy aroused, only a great propensity toward loving sincerity. Moreover, when he would tilt his muzzle to one side, his ears perked forward, falling in fluid flaps along his drooping chops, I understood how much the love one has for an animal is part of one's self-image; and I did not regret this, for in such moments he was utterly irresistible. And besides, there is no doubt that after a certain amount of cohabitation, man and beast borrow each other's failings. Rhett—who was, incidentally, rather poorly trained, that is to say not trained at all—was in fact afflicted with a pathology that hardly came as a surprise. If I qualified as gluttony the trait which ended up, in his case, more like obsessive bulimia, I would be falling far short of the truth. Just let a simple lettuce leaf fall to the floor, he would pounce upon it with an impressive nose dive that ended in a compact slide of his hindquarters, and then he would devour the leaf without even chewing it, in his fear of being tricked; I am convinced that it was only after the fact that he would identify what it was that he had caught. No doubt his motto was, Eat first, look later, and I often told myself that I was the owner of the only dog in the world who placed a higher price on his desire to eat than on the act of eating, for the greater part of his daily activity was spent in being there where he might *hope* to happen upon some revolting crumb. Though his ingeniousness did not extend to inventing subterfuges in order to procure some victuals, he was master of the art of placing himself strategically in the exact spot where a forgotten sausage might be lured away from the grill, or a crushed potato chip, vestige of a hasty before-dinner drink, might escape the attention of the masters of the house. What was more serious, his irrepressible passion for eating was eloquently (and somewhat dramatically) illustrated one Christmas in Paris, at my grandparents, where the meal, according to some antediluvian custom, must finish with a Yule log lovingly prepared by my grandmother, a simple rolled biscuit stuffed with a butter, coffee, or chocolate cream—it may have been a simple biscuit but it was laden with the magnificence of successful endeavors. Rhett was in fine fettle and frolicked his way around the apartment, gathering caresses here, being surreptitiously fed there with some treat carelessly dropped onto the carpet behind my father's back, and so, from the beginning of the meal, he had been making the rounds on a regular basis (corridor, living room, dining room, kitchen, corridor, and so on) where he engaged in not a few generous licking sessions. It was my father's sister Marie who first noticed his absence. I realized at the same time as the others that indeed for some time we had not noticed the recurring wag of the white, quivering plume above the armchairs, which was the sign that the dog was going by. After a short lapse of time during which we became brutally aware, my father, mother and I, of the probable turn of events, we leapt to our feet as if propelled by a single spring, and rushed to the bedroom where, as a precaution, because she knew the little rascal and his love of anything remotely culinary, my grandmother had stored the very precious dessert.

The bedroom door was open. Someone (the guilty party was never identified), despite all the admonishments in the matter, had forgotten to close the door, and the dog, whom one can hardly expect to single-handedly resist his own nature, had quite naturally concluded that the Yule log belonged to him. My mother let out a cry of despair: a white-tailed eagle in distress surely does not produce such wrenching cries. Rhett, in all probability too heavy from his spoils to react in his usual fashion, that is, by rushing through people's legs in order to reach a more benign refuge, stood there next to the empty plate watching us with a gaze devoid of all expression, all expectation fulfilled. Empty, in fact, is not exactly the right word. With methodical application, certain he would not be interrupted too soon, he had attacked the Yule log from right to left, then from left to right, and so on across its entire length, until we finally got there and all that was left of the sweet butter triumph was a thin, elongated filament, and it would have been futile indeed to hope that something might be recovered, to find its way onto our plates. Like Penelope unraveling the yarn on her loom, row upon row along its length, from a canvas that was meant to be a tapestry, Rhett had put his industrious fangs to good use in order to fashion a busy little shuttle, weaving the pleasure of his connoisseur's stomach.

My grandmother had such a good laugh that the incident was transformed from galactic catastrophe to savory anecdote. This was another aspect of the woman's talent, the way she could see the salt of life in situations where others might see nothing but inconvenience. She wagered that the dog would be the instrument of his own punishment by virtue of the monumental indigestion which the ingurgitation of a pastry intended for fifteen people could not fail to provoke without delay. She was proven wrong. Despite the suspicious protuberance which could be observed for several hours in the region of his belly, Rhett digested his

Christmas meal very well, aided by a deep siesta where he could be heard cooing with pleasure from time to time, and he was not even terribly indignant when the next morning he came upon his empty bowl, a paltry retaliatory measure implemented by my father who, to say the least, had not appreciated the display of mischief.

Is there a moral to the story? I briefly begrudged Rhett for having deprived me of a pleasure foretold. But I had also laughed wholeheartedly at the sight of the serene disrespect the dog had manifested toward the relentless labors of my dragon of a grandmother. And above all, there was one thought that had crossed my mind and which I had found very heartening. Seated around the table for the occasion were so many of my relatives for whom I felt, at best, scorn, at worst animosity, that in the end it seemed to me a delightful conclusion that the cake which had been destined for their dreary taste buds had delighted my dog's instead, for I am sure he had all the talents of a true gourmet. I am not, however, one of those people who prefer their dog to a stranger; a dog is nothing more than a thing that moves, barks and wiggles, while wandering through the province of our daily life. But if one must display one's disgust for those who deserve it, it may as well be done via these amusing furry beasts: they may be insignificant, but they are also marvelously adept at innocently conveying mockery, in spite of themselves.

A gift, a clown, a clone: he was all those things at once. He was funny, with his merry figure of soft refinement; he offered himself by radiating the unaffected kindness of his puppy soul; he was a clone of my own self, but then not altogether: I no longer saw the dog in him, any more than I made him into a man. He was Rhett, Rhett above all, before he was a dog, or an angel, or a beast, or a demon. But if I am speaking of him a few hours before my demise, it is because I have offended him by omitting him in my earlier evocation of natural fragrances. Indeed, Rhett was a source of olfactory delight all to himself. Yes, my dog, my Dalmatian exuded the most fantastic smell; and believe it or not, on his neck and on the top of his well-shaped crown he smelled like the toasty aroma of brioche bread with butter and cherry plum jam that would fill the kitchen in the morning. Thus, Rhett gave off the lovely smell of warm brioche, a yeasty fumet, which immediately made you want to sink your teeth in, and just picture this: all day long, the dog would frolic everywhere around the house and in the garden; whether he was trotting, supremely busy, from the living room to the study, or galloping to the far end of the field in a crusade against three presumptuous crows, or fidgeting in the kitchen in hopes of a tasty morsel, he always gave off the evocative aroma, and was thus a permanent living ode to the Sunday morning brioche: numb but content at the start of our day of rest, we would slip on a comfortable old cardigan and go down to make the coffee, one eye on the brown loaf sitting on the table. It's a delightful feeling to be not yet quite awake, taking a few silent moments to enjoy the fact of not being subjected to the laws of work, rubbing your eyes in a display of sympathy for yourself and, when the palpable aroma of hot coffee rises, you finally sit down before your steaming bowl and give a friendly squeeze to the brioche as you tear it apart, then you slowly bring a piece to the bowl of powdered sugar in the middle of the table and with your eyes half-closed you acknowledge—and no need to tell yourself as much—the bittersweet quality of happi-

ness. It is all of this that Rhett could evoke with his fragrant presence, and if I loved him as I did it was also surely for the way he came and went like some itinerant
boulangerie.

As I reminisce about Rhett, reliving these adventures I
haven't thought about in ages, there is one abandoned
aroma I have been able to recapture: that of warm and fragrant pastry, nestled in my dog's head. An aroma and
therefore other, similar, memories—mornings in America,
and the buttered toast that I used to gobble down,
astounded by the symbiosis between bread and butter
when they have been toasted *together.*

(Anna)

Rue de Grenelle, the Corridor

What is to become of me, my God, what is to become of me? I have no more strength, I cannot breathe, I have been emptied out, bled dry . . . I know that they don't understand, except Paul perhaps, I know what they are thinking . . . Jean, Laura, Clémence, where are you? Why this silence, why this distance, why all these misunderstandings, when we could have been so happy, the five of us? All you see is a cantankerous, authoritarian old man, you've never seen anyone but a tyrant, an oppressor, a despot who made life impossible for you, and for me—you set yourself up as knights in attendance who would console me in my distress as an abandoned wife and, in the end, I have not disabused you, I let you embellish my daily life with your laughter, as loving, comforting children, I have silenced my passion, silenced my reasons. I have silenced my own self.

I have always known what sort of life we would lead together. From the very first day, I could see that for him, far away from me, there would be banquets, and other women, and the career of a charmer with insane, miraculous talent; a prince, a lord constantly hunting outside his own walls, a man who, from one year to the next, would become ever more distant, would no longer even see me, would pierce my haunted soul with his falcon's eyes in order to embrace a view that was beyond my sight. I always knew this, and it didn't matter. The only thing that mattered were the times when he came back, and he always came back, and that was enough for me, I would be the woman to whom one returns unfailingly, however absentmindedly and vaguely. If you knew him, you would understand . . . If you knew the nights I have spent in his arms, trembling with excitement, transfixed with desire, crushed by his royal weight, his divine strength, I was happy, so happy, like the woman in love in her harem on the evenings when it is her turn, when she receives, reverently, the pearls of his gaze—because she lives for him alone, for his embrace, for his light. Perhaps he finds her tame, coy, childish; elsewhere, he has other lovers, tigresses, sensual felines, lustful panthers, with whom he roars with pleasure, in a debauchery of moans, of erotic gymnastics, and when it's all over, he feels as if he has reinvented the world, he is inflated with pride, with faith in his own virility—but, in fact, she takes her sensual pleasure on a deeper level, a mute pleasure, she gives herself, offers all of herself, receives religiously and it is in the silence of churches that she attains the pinnacle, almost without anyone noticing, because she has no need of anything else: his presence, his kisses. She is happy.

And so her children . . . she loves them, obviously. The joys of motherhood, of bringing them up, are things she has known; as well as the horror of having to raise children who are unloved by their father, the torture of watching them gradually learn to hate him, because he looks down on them, because he has abandoned her . . . But above all, she feels guilty because she loves them less than she loves him, because she was not able, was not willing to protect them from the man she was waiting for with all her waking energy, and there was no place left for anything else, no place left for them . . . If I had left, if I had been able to hate him too, then I might have saved them, they would have been released from the prison where I cast them, the prison of my resignation, of my mad desire for my own torturer . . . I raised my children to love their torturer . . . And today I am weeping tears of blood, because he is dying, he is leaving . . .

I remember how splendid we were, I held your arm, I was smiling in the gentle evening air, in my black silk gown, I was your wife and everyone was turning to look at us, murmuring, an appreciative whispering following in our footsteps, it followed us everywhere, like a light breeze, eternal . . . Don't die, please don't die . . . I love you . . .

Toast

Rue de Grenelle, the Bedroom

It was during a sojourn abroad occasioned by a seminar. I was already well known at the time, and I had been invited by the French community in San Francisco, where I chose to stay with a French journalist who lived near the Pacific Ocean, in a neighborhood to the southwest of the city. On the very first morning I was ravenous and my hosts were taking too long, for my liking, in their discussion about where to take me for "the breakfast of a lifetime." Through the open window, on a little prefab building, I could see a sign that said "John's Ocean Beach Cafe," and I decided it would be good enough for me.

From the start, I was beguiled by the door. The "open" sign, hanging on the frame from a little golden chain, went very well with the gleaming copper knob and made arrival in the café particularly welcoming, in an inexplicable way—it all made such an agreeable impression on me. But when I went into the main room, I was carried away. This was just as I had dreamt America would be, and despite all my expectations, flouting my certainty that once I was there I would revise all my clichés, it was exactly as I had imagined: a large rectangular room with wooden tables and booths covered in red leatherette; on the walls were photos of actors, a poster from *Gone with the Wind* with Scarlett and Rhett on the boat taking them to New

Orleans; a vast, well-polished wooden counter cluttered with butter, maple-syrup dispensers, and ketchup bottles. A blond waitress with a strong Slavic accent came over to us with her coffeepot in her hand; behind the bar, John, the chef, with his air of an Italian Mafioso, was busy grilling hamburgers with a disdainful sneer and a cynical expression. The interior of the café belied the exterior: everything bore a patina of age, worn furniture and a divine aroma of food frying. Oh, John! I had a look at the menu, chose the Scrambled Eggs with Sausage and John's Special Fries, and before long there arrived, in addition to a steaming cup of undrinkable coffee, a plate or rather a platter overflowing with scrambled eggs and potatoes sautéed in garlic, topped with three greasy little aromatic sausages, while the pretty Russian waitress set down next to all this a smaller plate piled with buttered toast, accompanied by a pot of blueberry jam. People say Americans are fat because they eat too much and eat badly. This is true, but in this incrimination one should not include their gargantuan breakfasts. I am inclined to think that, on the contrary, they are exactly what a man needs to face the day, and our stingy little French breakfasts—given the spinelessness clearly imbued with snobbery with which anything salty or porky is shunned—constitute an insult to the requisites of the body.

The moment I bit into the slice of toast, utterly sated for having honored my bountiful plate up to the very last morsel, I was overcome with an inexpressible sense of well-being. Why is it that in France we obstinately refrain from buttering our bread until after it has been toasted? The reason the two entities should be subjected together to the flickering flame is that in this intimate moment of burning they attain an unequalled complicity. The butter loses some of its creamy consistency, but nevertheless is not as liquid as when it is melted on its own, in a bain-marie or a saucepan. Likewise, the toast is spared a some-what dreary dryness, and becomes a moist, warm sub-stance, neither sponge nor bread but something in between, ready to tantalize one's taste buds with its con-templative delicacy.

It is terrible how close I feel. Bread, brioche . . . it seems that at last I am headed down the right path, the one which will lead to my truth. Or have I been induced in error yet again—the wrong track leading me astray, con-vincing me all the better to disappoint me, to laugh sar-castically at my undoing? I shall try other alternatives. Time to take a gamble.

(Rick)

Rue de Grenelle, the Bedroom

S o here I am, basking in my basket, or sprawled on the sofa feeling feline—have you ever seen such purrfect style?!

My name is Rick. My master is generally inclined to assign names from the movies to his pets, but I will hasten to point out that I am his favorite. Indeed I am. There have been many cats here over the years: a few of them unfortunately were not robust enough and they quickly disappeared, others were victims of tragic accidents (like the year they had to replace the drainpipe that gave way under the weight of a very sweet little white cat called Scarlett), and there were others with greater longevity, but now I am the only one left, and here I am, nineteen years I've knocked about as head tomcat on the Persian rugs of my abode; just me, the favorite, the master's alter ego, the one and only, to whom he declared his thoughtful, undying love one day when I was stretched out on the desk across his latest restaurant review, beneath the big warm lamp. "Rick," he said, ruffling the fur at the base of my spine, "Rick, you're my favorite, oh yes, what a fine cat you are, aren't you, now . . . I'm not mad at you, you can even tear up this paper, I'll never get mad at you . . . who's a fine tom with his buccaneer's whiskers . . . his silky fur . . . look at those Olympian muscles . . . that Herculean back . . . those iridescent opal eyes . . . yes, my fine kitty . . . my one and only . . . "

Why Rick? you may ask. I myself often wondered, but as I have no words with which to formulate the question, it went unheeded until one December evening about ten years ago, when a little redheaded woman, who used to come to the house to have tea with the Maître, asked, as she gently stroked my neck, where my name had come from. (I liked her, that lady, she always had a slightly musky fumet about her, very unusual for a woman, as most of her sex are inevitably smeared with heavy, heady perfumes, lacking that little scent of venison in which a cat— a real cat—can find just what he's looking for.) He replied, "It's after the character Rick in *Casablanca*, he's a man who knows how to give up a woman because he would rather have his freedom." I could sense that she stiffened a little. But I could also appreciate that aura of manly seduction with which the Maître gratified me through his offhand reply.

Of course today none of that matters anymore. Today the Maître is going to die. I know he is, I heard Chabrot tell him so, and when he had left, the Maître took me on his lap, looked me in the eyes (they must really have been pitiful, my poor tired eyes, and it's not because cats don't cry that they don't know how to show they are sad), and he said, sorrowfully, "Never listen to doctors, sweetheart." But I can see that it's the end. His, and mine, because I've always known we would have to die together. And so while his right hand is on my docile tail and I've got my pads planted on the plumped comforter, I can reminisce.

It was always like this. I could hear his quick steps on the tiles in the entrance, and very soon he'd be coming up the steps two by two. I would instantly jump up onto my velvet paws and make a beeline for the hall and there, on the somewhat ochre kilim, between the coat rack and the marble console, I would wait obediently.

He would open the door, remove his overcoat, hang it up with an abrupt gesture, see me at last and then lean over to caress me with a smile. Anna would arrive quickly thereafter, but he didn't look at her, and he went on stroking me, gently petting me. "Has he lost weight, the cat, do you think, Anna?" he would ask, a touch of concern in his voice. "Of course not, dearest, of course not." I would follow him into his study, then perform his favorite number (crouch down, leap and land noiselessly, as soft as leather, on the morocco-bound blotter). "Good boy, come over here, come and tell me everything that's happened all this time . . . Nyes . . . I've got the devil's own amount of work here . . . but you don't care and you're absolutely right . . . mmm, feel that silky little belly . . . there, stretch out over there so I can get some work done . . . "

Never again will there be the scratching of his pen on the white sheet, never again those afternoons with the rain pounding on the windowpane, while next to him in the muffled comfort of his impenetrable study I would grow languid, faithfully accompanying the gestation of his grandiose oeuvre. Never again.

Whisky

Rue de Grenelle, the Bedroom

My grandpa had been in the war with him. They hadn't had much to say to each other since that memorable time, but it had sealed between them an indestructible friendship which would not cease even upon my grandfather's death. Gaston Bienheureux—that was his name—would continue to visit his friend's widow for as long as she was still alive, and went so far as to display the silent tact of dying a few weeks after she did, his task accomplished.

Sometimes he came to Paris on business and he never failed to stop off at his friend's with a little crate of the latest vintage. But twice a year, at Easter and All Saint's Day, it was grandpa who "went down" to Burgundy, alone, without his wife, for three days which we assumed were well-watered, and he was always taciturn upon his return, deigning only to articulate that they had "had a good talk."

When I was fifteen he took me with him. Burgundy is reputed above all for its wines from the Côte, the narrow verdant strip of land which stretches from Dijon to Beaune through an impressive palette of prestigious names: Gevrey-Chambertin, Nuits-Saint-Georges, Aloxe-Corton, and, further south, Pommard, Monthélie, and Meursault, almost exiled to the border of the county. Gaston Bien-heureux was not one to envy those well-off sorts. In Irancy he was born, in Irancy he lived, in Irancy he would die. In this little village in the Yonne region, nestled in a farandole of hills and entirely devoted to the grape which prospers in its generous soil, there is no envy of faraway neighbors, for the nectar lovingly produced there does not seek competition. It knows its strengths, it has its qualities: there is nothing more it needs in order to endure.

The French are often, when it comes to wine, so formal that they border on the ridiculous. My father had taken me, several months earlier, to visit the cellars of the Château de Meursault: so much splendor! The arches and vaulted ceilings, the pomp of the labels, the coppered gleam of the racks, and the crystal glasses all spoke for the quality of the wine, but were hindrances to my pleasure upon tasting it. All these luxurious intrusions of décor and decorum were interferences, and I could not determine whether it was the liquid or the surroundings that were teasing my tongue with an extravagant stimulus. To be honest, I was not yet terribly sensitive to the charms of wine, but I was only too aware that a man of quality is obliged to appreciate tasting it on a daily basis, and so, in the hopes that things would eventually head down the right path, I confessed to no one that all I gleaned from the exercise was a very mediocre satisfaction. Since that time, naturally, I have been inducted into the brotherhood of wine, I have come to understand—and reveal to others— the power of a full-bodied vintage pulsating in one's mouth, flooding it with a bouquet of tannin where the flavor is increased tenfold. But at the time I was too immature to measure up to wine, and I drank it somewhat reticently, waiting impatiently for it to share with me the talents for which it is renowned. Therefore, what I looked forward to in my grandpa's treat was not so much the alcoholic promises it concealed as the pleasure of his company and the discovery of an unfamiliar countryside.

From the start I liked the landscape, but also Gaston's wine cellar, a place without frills, a simple large damp cellar with a beaten-earth floor and cob walls. Here there were neither vaults nor arches; nor was there a château to greet the customer, only a pretty Burgundian house blooming with courtesy and discreet by vocation; a few ordinary stem glasses placed on a barrel at the entrance to the cellar. That is where, no sooner had we stepped out of the car, we began our tasting.

How they talked, on and on. Glass after glass, as they went through the bottles the winemaker opened one after the other, with total disregard for the spittoons placed here and there in the room for those who wanted to taste without fear of getting drunk; they drank methodically, accompanying the purely phatic rehashing of clearly imaginary memories with impressive amounts of liquid. I was no longer feeling very robust myself when Gaston, who thus far had only acknowledged me somewhat absentmindedly, looked me over more sharply and said to my grandfather, "The lad doesn't care for wine much, now, does he?" I was too tipsy to protest my innocence. What's more, with his overalls, wide black suspenders, red plaid shirt as bright as his nose and cheeks, and his black beret, I really liked the man, and didn't want to lie to him. So I did not contradict him.

Every man, in his way, is master of his castle. The coarsest peasant, the most uncultured winemaker, the most miserable employee, the shabbiest shopkeeper, the greatest pariah among all those who have been excluded from the consideration of society, rejected lock stock and barrel; the simplest of men, therefore, always have in their possession their very own genius, the one that will ensure them of their hour of glory. All the more so someone like Gaston, who was not a pariah. This simple worker, who may have been a prosperous tradesman but remained a peasant at heart, isolated on his few acres of vineyard, suddenly became for me a prince among princes, because in any activity, whether noble or reviled, there is always room for an all-powerful flash of realization.

"Shouldn't you teach him something about life, Albert?" he asked. "Do you think the kid would be up for some DTH?" And my grandfather laughed quietly. "You see, lad," continued Gaston, inspired by the imminent prospect of furthering my education, "everything you've tasted here today is good stuff, the real thing. But a wine-maker doesn't sell everything: as you might suspect, he keeps some stuff for himself, for his thirst, not for trade (his good-natured mug was split ear to ear by a smile worthy of a crafty fox). So he always keeps some DTH on hand, some 'down the hatch.' And when he has people round, friends, I should say, well, he dips into his DTH." He suddenly interrupted the tippling that was already well in progress. "Come away here, come on then," he said impatiently, as I rose unsteadily to my feet. Giving him a grim look, my tongue coated with the devious ways of drink, I followed him to the back of the cellar and, although I was greatly intrigued by this new concept, the DTH, which was bound to offer undreamt-of glimpses into the lifestyle of gentlemen of taste, I expected it to lead to still more glug-glugging of wine, a prospect that filled me with a certain amount of apprehension. "Since you're

still a bit on the young side for the serious things of life,"
he continued, stopping in front of a massive cupboard
armed with an enormous padlock, "and with the parents
you have, you can't expect too much either"—he slipped
my grandfather a gaze that left no doubt about what he
was implying, and Albert said not a word—"to my way of
thinking it's time to clean out your pipe with something a
bit more astringent. What I'm going to dig out here for
you from behind the firewood is something I'm sure
you've never drunk. It's good stuff. This will be your bap-
tism. I'll say it again: you're in for a true education."

Out of an unfathomably deep pocket he pulled a very
heavy set of keys, put one of them into the enormous lock,
and turned. My grandpa's expression instantly became
more serious. Warned by this sudden solemnity, I sniffed
nervously, straightened my spine, which had become seri-
ously impaired by our tippling, and waited with consider-
able apprehension while Gaston, with a meaningful gesture, took from the safe a bottle wrapped in black that most
definitely was not wine, and a large, squat, unadorned
glass.

This was the DTH. He ordered his whisky from Scot-
land, from one of the best distilleries in the country. The
owner was a chap he'd known in Normandy, just after the
war, and with whom he'd quickly discovered a shared
affinity for liquids rated by degrees. Every year a crate of
the precious whisky came to join the handful of bottles of
wine he put aside for personal use. And from varietals to
peat, from ruby to amber, and from alcohol to alcohol, he
reconciled the two before and during meals that he himself qualified as profoundly European.

"I sell some good things, but the best go down my

hatch." The way he treated the few bottles set aside from the grape harvest, and his friend Mark's whisky (to his regular guests he only served a very good whisky bought locally, which was to the Scotsman's whisky what a tomato in a can is to its rival in the vegetable garden), caused him to rise all at once in my adolescent's esteem, which already assumed that greatness and expertise are to be measured by exceptions and not by rules, even if they were rules made by kings. With his private little cellar Gaston Bienheureux had just become, in my eyes, a potential artist. Subsequently I never failed to suspect all the restaurateurs in whose establishments I dined of displaying on their tables no more than the minor works of their industry, and of keeping for themselves, in the intimacy of their culinary alcoves, victuals that were worthy of a pantheon and inaccessible to ordinary mortals. But for the moment I was hardly preoccupied by such philosophical consideration. I stared dumbly at the bronze liquid as he poured out a meager portion and, filled with misgivings, I sought in my deepest soul the courage to confront it.

To start with, the unfamiliar aroma unsettled me beyond anything I thought possible. Such formidable aggressiveness, such a muscular, abrupt explosion, dry and fruity at the same time, like a charge of adrenaline that has deserted the tissues where it ordinarily resides in order to evaporate upon the surface of the nose, a gaseous concentration of sensorial precipices . . . Stunned, I discovered that I liked this blunt whiff of incisive fermentation.

Like some ethereal marchioness, I cautiously ventured my lips into the peaty magma and . . . what a violent effect! An explosion of piquancy and seething elements suddenly detonates in my mouth; my organs no longer exist, no more palate or cheeks or saliva, only the ravaging sensation that some telluric warfare is raging inside me. In raptures, I allowed the first mouthful to linger for a moment on my tongue, while concentric undulations continued to engage it for a long while. That is the first way to drink whisky: absorb it ferociously, inhaling its pungent, unforgiving taste. The second swallow, on the other hand, was undertaken precipitously; as soon as it had gone down, it took a moment to warm my solar plexus—but what warmth it was! The stereotypical gesture of the man who drinks strong liquor—swallowing down the object of his desire in one gulp, then waiting, then closing his eyes from the shock and exhaling a sigh of mingled ease and commotion—offers a second manner of drinking whisky, where the taste buds are almost insensitive because the alcohol is merely passing through one's throat, and the plexus, perfectly sensitive, is suddenly overwhelmed by heat as if a bomb of ethylic plasma had landed there. It heats, and heats again, it disconcerts and rouses. It feels good. It is a sun whose blessed rays assure the body of its beaming presence.

Thus it was in the heart of wine-growing Burgundy that I drank my first whisky and experienced for the first time the power it has to wake the dead. With this added irony: the fact that Gaston himself led me to this discovery should have put me on the path of my true passion. Yet throughout my career I have never considered whisky to be anything more than a drink which, however delightful, is nevertheless of secondary importance: only the gold of wine could deserve my praise and the most significant prophecies of my oeuvre. Alas . . . it is only now that I understand: wine is the refined jewel that only a grown woman will prefer to the sparkling glossy trinkets adored by little girls. I learned to love what was worthy but in doing so I neglected to entertain the sudden passion that had no need of education. I truly love only beer and whisky—even though I do acknowledge that wine is divine. And as it has been decreed that today will be little more than a long series of acts of contrition, here is yet another: oh, Mephistophelean whisky, I loved you from the first swig, and betrayed you from the second—but nowhere else did I ever find, amidst the tyranny of flavors imposed upon me by my position, such a nuclear expansion capable of blasting my jaw away with delight . . .

Desolation: I have been laying siege to my lost flavor in the wrong citadel . . . It is not to be found in the wind or heather of a desolate moor, nor in a deep loch or a dark stone wall. All of that is lacking in indulgence, in affability, in moderation. Ice, not fire: I find myself trapped at the wrong impasse.

(Laure)

Nice

*O**n est bien peu de chose, et mon amie la rose me l'a dit ce matin* . . . My God, what a sad song . . . I am sad myself . . . and weary, so weary . . .

I was born in an old French family where values still remain what they have always been. A family of granite rigidity. It would never have crossed my mind that these values might be questioned: an idiotic and old-fashioned youth—somewhat romantic, somewhat diaphanous—spent waiting for Prince Charming and exhibiting my cameo profile whenever a worldly occasion arose. And then I got married, and quite naturally it meant the passage from the protection of my parents to that of my husband, and the dashing of my hopes, and the insignificance of life as a woman kept back in childhood, a life devoted to bridge parties and receptions for want of anything better to do, utterly unaware that there might actually be something better to do.

And then I met him. I was still young and beautiful, a slender doe, too easy a prey. The excitement of clandestinity, the adrenaline of adultery, the fever of forbidden sex: I had found my prince, I had drugged my life, on the sofa I played my role, languishing and lovely, I let him admire my willowy, racy beauty, at last I was alive, I existed, and in his eyes I became a goddess, I became Venus.

Of course, he really didn't want anything to do with a sentimental little girl. What for me had been transgression was for him merely futile entertainment, a charming distraction. Indifference is far more cruel than hatred: from non-being I had come, to non-being I would return. To my sullen husband, to my bleary frivolousness, to the eroticism of an innocent young thing, to the empty thoughts of a graceful silly goose: my cross to bear, my Waterloo.

Let him die, then.

Ice Cream

Rue de Grenelle, the Bedroom

What I liked about Marquet was her generosity. She didn't seek to innovate at any cost—a tactic many great chefs resort to in order to ward off the criticism that they are afraid of change—and while she did not rest on her laurels with her existing accomplishments, she only worked relentlessly because, in the end, it was her nature, and she liked what she was doing. Thus, when dining in her restaurant, you could just as easily romp your way through a menu that was perpetually youthful as order a dish from an earlier era, which she would prepare with all the good grace of a prima donna cajoled through flattery to provide an encore of one of the arias that made her famous.

I had been feasting at her place for twenty years. Of all the great chefs I have had the honor of frequenting on intimate terms, she was the only one who truly embodied my ideal of creative perfection. She never disappointed me: her dishes always baffled me to the bone, to the point of inducing a fit, perhaps precisely because her even touch and the originality of her perpetually inventive provender came so naturally.

That July evening, I had sat down at a table outdoors, as overexcited as a mischievous child. The Marne was lapping gently at my feet. The white stone of the old restored mill, halfway between land and river, eaten away in places by a soft green moss that found its way into the slightest crack, was glowing gently in the early darkness. Before long, the terraces would be lit. I have always had a particular fondness for the fertile countryside, where a river, a spring, or a stream, flowing across the meadow, confers upon the surroundings the serenity of uliginous atmospheres. A house by the water: crystalline tranquility, the lure of still water, the mineral indifference of waterfalls, no sooner here than gone again, serving forthwith to make all human concerns seem relative. But on that particular day, I felt incapable of savoring the charms of the place, almost reclusive, and I waited with relative patience for the mistress of the premises to arrive. Which she did almost at once.

"Well," I said, "this evening I would like a rather particular supper." And I enumerated my requests.

Menu. 1982. *A Royal of Sea urchin with Sansho, saddle of hare, rabbit kidneys and liver with winkles. Buckwheat pancake.* 1979: *Cod in an agria macaire; violet maco from the Midi; plump Gillardeau oysters and grilled foie gras. Mackerel bouillon laced with leeks.* 1989: *Thick chunks of turbot cooked in a casserole with aromatic herbs, deglazed with homemade cider. Quarters of Comice pears with cucumber greens.* 1996: *Pastis of Gauthier pigeon with mace, dried fruit and foie gras with radishes.* 1988: *Madeleines with tonka beans.*

It was an anthology. In one single clutch of eternity I had gathered together that which years of culinary spiritedness had created in the way of timeless blandishments: from the shapeless accumulation of dishes I was extracting a handful of veritable nuggets, the contiguous pearls of a goddess's necklace, in order to make them into a work of legend.

A moment of triumph. She looked at me for an instant, flabbergasted, the time it took to *understand;* lowered her gaze onto my empty, waiting plate; then, slowly, training an ever so appreciative gaze upon me—full of praise, admiring, and respectful all at the same time, she nodded her head and puckered her lips in a pout of deferential homage. "Well yes, of course," she said. "Of course, it's proof that . . . "

Naturally, it was a feast worthy of an anthology, and it was perhaps the only time during our long cohabitation as food lovers that we were truly united in the fervor of a meal, neither critic nor cook, only high-flying connoisseurs sharing their allegiance to a same emotion. But while this memory of noble lineage may flatter above all my self-importance as a creator, that is not the reason why I have caused it to re-emerge from the mists of my unconsciousness.

Madeleines of tonka beans, or the art of the offhand shortcut! It would be an insult to assume that a dessert chez Marquet could consist of nothing more than setting a few skinny madeleines set on a plate and sprinkled with beans. The pastry was hardly more than a pretext, that of a psalm—sweet, honeyed, fondant and dripping, where, in the mad confusion of cookies, candied fruits, icings, crêpes, chocolate, sabayons, red berries, ice creams and sorbets, a progressive passage from hot to cold was being explored by my expert tongue: it clucked with compulsive satisfaction, it danced a devilish jig at the merriest of balls. I favored ice cream and sorbet, in particular. I adore ice cream: frozen cream saturated with milk, fat, artificial flavors, bits of fruit, coffee beans, rum; Italian gelati solid as velvet spiraled with vanilla, strawberry or chocolate; ice cream sundaes crumbling under the weight of whipped cream, peaches, almonds and coulis of all sorts; simple popsicles with a coating that is crunchy, fine and firm all at once, that you eat in the street between two appointments, or in the evening in summer in front of the television, when it has become clear that this is the only way to make yourself feel a little cooler, a little less thirsty; and finally the sorbets, the triumphant synthesis of ice and fruit, robust refreshment that evaporates in your mouth in a glacier's flow. The plate that had been set down in front of me contained examples of her industry: one was a tomato sorbet, another was classical, with wild berries and fruit, and a third one, finally, was orange.

In the simple word "sorbet," there is an entire world. Try saying this out loud: "Would you like an ice cream?" then immediately following with "What about a sorbet?" and notice the difference. It's a bit like saying, as you open the door, in an offhand way, "I'm going out to buy a cake," whereas you could very well, without being so casual or banal, have ventured, "I'm going to get some patisseries" (and mind you detach each syllable: not "patisseries" but "pa-tis-*se*-ries"), and, with the magic of a somewhat outdated, precious word you can create, at lesser cost, a world of old-world harmony. Thus, if you suggest "sorbet" where others might merely be thinking "ice cream" (which, very often, for the layman includes preparations made from milk or water), you have already opted for lightness, already chosen refinement, you are offering airy vistas while refusing a heavy land-bound trek with closed horizons. Airy, indeed: a sorbet is airy, almost immaterial, it froths ever so slightly as it makes contact with your warmth and then, vanquished, squeezed, liquefied, it evaporates down your throat and all it leaves on the tongue is the charming reminiscence of the fruit and water which once flowed there.

Thus I set upon the orange sorbet, tasted it as a man in the know, certain of what I was about to discover but attentive all the same to what were ever-changing sensations. And then something stopped me. I had tasted the other iced waters with the peace of mind of one who knows his stuff. But this sorbet, this orange one, was a cut above all the others, with its extravagant texture, its excessive aqueousness, as if someone had just filled a little bowl with a bit of water and a squeezed orange which had then been placed in the freezer for the regulation amount of time, producing these fragrant icy chunks, lumpy just as any impure liquid one tries to freeze can be, and which remind us strongly of the taste of the crumbly crushed snow we ate as children, with our hands, on days when the sky was a deep cold and we were playing outdoors. That was also my grandmother's approach in the summer when at times it was so hot that I would tuck my head into the door of the freezer and, sweating and cursing, she would twist heavy dripping rags around her neck, which also served to slay a few lazy flies stuck together in places they shouldn't be. When the ice had set, she would turn the basin over, shake it vigorously above a bowl, crush the orangey mass and serve us a ladleful in a large goblet we would seize as if it were a holy relic. And I realized that, in the end, all this banquet was for one thing alone: to reach the moment of the *sorbet à l'orange*, my childhood stalactites; to feel, tonight of all nights, the worth and truth of my gastronomic attachments.

Later, in the half darkness, I asked Marquet in a whisper, "How do you do it, your sorbet, the sorbet à l'orange?"

She turned halfway on the pillow; light locks of hair curled around my shoulder.

"The way my grandmother does," she answered, with a brilliant smile.

I'm nearly there. Fire . . . ice. Cream!

(Marquet)

Maison Marquet, near Meaux

No doubt about it, he was a regular bastard. He has consumed both my self and my cuisine with the presumptuousness of a common boor, as if it were only natural for Marquet to bow down before him, offering her dishes and her buttocks from the very first visit . . . A regular bastard, but we had some good times together, and that's something he can't take away from me, because what is mine, for good, is the thrill of conversing with a true genius of the food world, and of taking my pleasure with an exceptional lover; and still I remain a free woman, a proud woman . . .

Still, if he had been free, and if he had been the sort of man who might make of a woman something other than a tart available all hours of the day—who knows . . . But then he wouldn't have been the same man, would he?

Mayonnaise

Rue de Grenelle, the Bedroom

There is nothing more delightful than to see the order of the world bend to one's desires. Such is the unprecedented license to penetrate a temple of haute cuisine in the unbridled felicity of being able to taste each and every dish. The hidden frisson when the maître d' draws near with muffled footsteps; his impersonal gaze, a fragile yet successful compromise between respect and discretion, is a tribute to one's social capital. You are nobody because you are somebody; here, no one will spy on you, no one will try to pigeonhole you. The fact that you have been allowed to enter the premises is proof enough of who you are. A modest little tug at the heart as you open the menu, printed on a grainy vellum like a damask napkin of yore. Your astonishment expertly tempered as you feel your way for the first time through the whispered offer of dishes. Your gaze slips, refuses for a while to be caught by any particular ode, merely catches a few voluptuous fragments on the wing, frolics about in the luxurious profusion of terms you seize upon at random. Culotte of baby veal . . . pistachio cassata . . . wedge of angler fish on a bed of scampi . . . galinette de palangre . . . au naturel . . . amber gelée with eggplant . . . seasoned with Cremona mustard . . . a confit of shallots . . . marinière of poached bass . . . iced sabayon . . . blue lobster . . . breast of Peking duck . . . A first nibble of ecstasy at last when the magic takes over and devours your attention with a single line:

Pan-roasted breast of Peking duck rubbed with berbère; grapefruit crumble à la Jamaïque with a confit of shallots.

You repress any untimely salivation, your ability to concentrate has reached its summit. You are in possession of the symphony's dominant note.

It is not so much the duck or its berbère and grapefruit which have electrified you in this way, even if they are glazed with the promise of a dish whose key is sunny, spicy, and sweet, and whose hues range from almond to bronze to gold. But the confit of shallots, instantly aromatic and fondant, pricking your still-virgin tongue with the anticipated savor of a mélange of fresh ginger, marinated onion and musk, is titillating your appetite—and this is all it wants, after all—with its refinement and extravagance. On its own, however, this dish would not have been decisive; it required the incomparable poetry of "pan-roasted," evoking in an olfactory cascade the fumet of fowl grilled in the open air at a cattle market, the sensorial pandemonium of Chinese bazaars, the irresistible conjunction of crispness and succulence when the meat is firm and juicy inside its crusty skin, the familiar mystery of the pan itself, neither a spit nor a grill, lulling the duck as it cooks; all of this is required, and the combination of odor and taste, to determine your choice on this particular day. All that remains is to embroider upon the theme.

How many times have I immersed myself in a menu the way one immerses oneself in the unknown? It would be pointless to try to work out such a figure. Every time, I have found my pleasure intact. But never has it been as acute as on that day when, by the stoves of the chef Lessière, in the holy of holies of gastronomic exploration, I turned away from a menu whose delights were deafening to wallow in the debauchery of simple mayonnaise.

I had dipped my finger into it, casually, in passing, the way you let your hand trail in fresh water from a drifting boat. We were talking together about his new menu, it was afternoon, between two waves of fellow diners, and in his kitchen I felt just as I used to in my grandmother's: I was a familiar stranger, allowed into the harem. What I tasted surprised me. This was indeed mayonnaise, and that was precisely what troubled me; a sheep that has lost its way amidst a pride of lions, this traditional condiment looked utterly and ridiculously archaic. "What is this?" I asked, implying, how did a simple homemaker's mayonnaise end up here? "Well, it's mayonnaise," he replied with a laugh. "Don't tell me you don't know what mayonnaise is." "Mayonnaise just like that, the basic recipe?" I was quite unnerved "Yes, the basic one. I don't know of any better way to make it. An egg, some oil, salt and pepper." I insisted. "And what is it meant to go with?" He looked at me carefully. "I'll tell you," he replied slowly, "I'll tell you what it is meant to go with." He ordered a kitchen boy to bring him some vegetables and some cold pork roast, and set about his task at once, peeling the vegetables. I had forgotten, I had forgotten that in his position as *maître d'oeuvre* and not critic he was obliged never to forget what we wrongly refer to as "the basics" of cooking, and which comprise, if anything, the essential framework, and he had taken it upon himself to remind me, through a somewhat scornful lesson that he was giving to me as a favor—for critics and chefs are like dishrags and napkins: they complement each other, spend time together, work together, but in their heart of hearts, they do not like one another.

Carrots, celery, cucumbers, tomatoes, bell peppers, radishes, cauliflower and broccoli: he had cut them all lengthwise, or at any rate those that he could cut lengthwise, in other words all but the last two which, although flowery, could be taken by the stem, somewhat in the manner with which one grabs hold of the hilt of a sword. To all this he added a few thin slices of pork roast, cold and succulent. We began to dip.

No one will ever manage to banish from my thoughts the notion that raw food with mayonnaise is somehow deeply sexual. The hard vegetable insinuating its way into the unctuousness of the cream; unlike many other preparations, here there is no chemistry causing each of the two foodstuffs to sacrifice a part of its nature and espouse that of the other, thus becoming through osmosis, like bread and butter, a new and wonderful substance. In this case, mayonnaise and vegetables remain perennial, each identical to its own self but, as in the carnal act, hopelessly ecstatic at being together. As for the meat, it nevertheless does obtain something more: its texture is elastic and porous, it yields to the bite and fills with mayonnaise in such a way that what one is chewing on, without false modesty, is something firm at heart that has been drizzled with a velvety moisture. Add to this the delicacy of a smooth flavor, for there is nothing biting about mayonnaise, no hot spiciness—like water, it surprises one's mouth with its affable neutrality; then come the exquisite nuances of the spread of vegetables: insolent tang of radishes and cauliflower, watery sweetness of the tomato, discreet acidity of broccoli, generosity of the carrot upon the tongue, the crunchy licorice hints of celery . . . a treat fit for a king.

But just as I am recalling this incongruous meal—it was like a summer picnic by the woods, one of those perfect days where the sun is shining, there is a gentle breeze, and life seems to be decked out in clichés—a new memory has come to supersede it, and my reminiscences are suddenly illuminated with a deep authenticity, causing a turbulence of emotions to rise in my heart like bubbles of air forcing their way to the surface of the water which, when they break free, will explode in a chorus of bravos. For my mother—who, as I have already pointed out, was a pathetic cook—also served us mayonnaise, and quite often at that, although her mayonnaise came in a glass jar from the supermarket; despite this insult to truly discerning taste, it nevertheless led to an unshakeable preference. While one might mourn the tasty, homemade touch necessary to produce pure mayonnaise, processed mayonnaise offers one characteristic that is lacking in the real thing, and the best chef must, sooner or later, concede the bitter truth: even the most homogeneous and unctuous of condiments tends, very quickly, to break up a bit, slowly disintegrating, oh, only ever so slightly, but nevertheless enough for the consistency of the cream to be marred by a very slight contrast, which will cause it to abandon, in the most microscopic way, its initial state, which was utterly and absolutely smooth, as smooth as can be—whereas supermarket mayonnaise avoids any viscosity. There is no texture, there are no elements, no components, and that is what I loved passionately, that taste of nothing, that substance without backbone, offering no hold with which to circumvent it as it slid along my tongue with the fluidity of something soluble.

Yes, that's it, I'm nearly there. Between the breast of Peking duck and the ointment in a jar, between the lair of a genius and the grocery store shelf, I would choose the latter, I would choose the horrid little supermarket where the guilty objects of my delight were lined up in dreary, uniform rows. The supermarket . . . Odd how this is stirring a wave of emotion . . . Yes, perhaps . . . perhaps . . .

(Paul)

Rue de Grenelle, the Corridor

S uch a waste.
He has crushed everything in his wake. Everything.
His children, his wife, his mistresses, even his own
creative work: now in his final hours he is rejecting them
all, because of this request that he himself does not understand, but which is tantamount to a condemnation of his
science and a denunciation of everything he once stood
for, a request he has addressed to us like a beggar, like a
ragged pauper by the roadside, deprived of any meaningful life, alienated from his own understanding—wretched,
in the end, because he has realized in this moment among
all others, that he has been chasing a chimera and preaching a false gospel. A flavor . . . What do you think, old
madman, what do you think? That if you find a lost flavor
you will eradicate decades of misunderstanding and find
yourself confronted with a truth that might redeem the
aridity of your heart of stone? And yet he had in his possession all the arms that make for the best duelist: a fine
way with his pen, nerve, panache. His prose . . . his prose
was nectar, ambrosia, a hymn to language: it was gut-
wrenching, and it hardly mattered whether he was talking
about food or something else, it would be a mistake to
think that the topic mattered: it was the way he phrased it
that was so brilliant. Food was just a pretext, perhaps even

a way of escaping, of fleeing what his goldsmith's talent might bring to light: the exact tenor of his emotions, the harshness and suffering, and the failure, in the end . . . Thus, where his genius might have enabled him to dissect for posterity and for himself the various feelings which were troubling him, he lost his way along secondary paths, convinced that he ought to say what was incidental, and not essential. Such a waste. Heartbreaking.

And as for me . . . obsessed as he was with his sham success, he did not see who I really am. Neither the striking contrast between my ambitions as a hotheaded young man and the life as a quiet notable that I lead against my will; nor my stubborn tendency to muddle our conversation, to hide the inhibitions of a sad childhood beneath a ceremonial cynicism, to join him in performing a farce that may have seemed brilliant but was really nothing more than an illusion. Paul, the prodigal nephew, the favorite child— favorite because he had dared to refuse, dared to break the tyrant's laws, dared to speak loud and clear in his presence where others whispered: but, old madman, even the most turbulent, even the most violent, the most rebellious of sons cannot be all those things without the formal authorization of the father, and yet again it is the father who, for a reason unbeknownst to himself, *needs* this troublemaker, needs to have this spine planted in the heart of his home, needs this small refuge of opposition, a place where, in the end, all the oversimplified categories of will and character shall be proven wrong. I was your damned soul for the simple reason that it is what you wanted, and how many sensible young men could have resisted such a temptation—to become the flattered foil to a universal demiurge, taking on the role of opponent that he had created specially for them? Old madman, old madman . . . You scorn Jean, you praise me to the skies, and yet we are both little other than the product of your desire—with the only difference that Jean is dying because of it, whereas I delight in it and make the most of it.

But it is too late now, too late to speak truthfully, to save what might have been saved. I am not enough of a Christian to believe in conversion, let alone last-minute conversion, and for my expiation I will live with the burden of my cowardice, that of having played at being what I am not, until for me, too, death does ensue.

I'll speak to Jean all the same.

The Illumination

Rue de Grenelle, the Bedroom

Then suddenly I remember. Tears flow from my eyes. I murmur frenetically a few words incomprehensible to those around me, I am weeping and laughing at the same time, I raise my arms and trace circles convulsively with my hands. Around me everyone is agitated, concerned. I know I must look like what I am, basically: a mature man on his deathbed, who has lapsed into infancy as he prepares to depart his life. With a Dantean effort I manage to restrain my excitement for a short spell—a titanic struggle against my own jubilation, because I absolutely must make myself clear.

"My . . . little . . . Paul," I manage to utter, with difficulty, "my . . . little . . . Paul . . . do . . . something . . . for . . . me."

He is leaning over me, his nose almost touching mine, his brows, frowning with anxiety, form an admirable motif around his distraught blue eyes, and his entire body is tense with the effort to understand me.

"Yes, yes, uncle," he says. "What do you want, what do you want?"

"Go . . . buy me . . . some . . . chouquettes," I say, realizing with horror that the exultation flooding my soul as I utter these marvelous words could usher me brutally out of this world before it is time. I stiffen, expecting the worst, but nothing happens. I catch my breath.

"Chouquettes? You want some chouquettes?"

I nod, smiling faintly. A trace of a smile forms gently on his lips.

"So that's what you want, you old madman, some chouquettes?" He squeezes my arm affectionately. "I'll go get some. I'll leave right away."

I can see Anna behind him, coming to life, and I hear her say, "Go to Lenôtre, it's the closest."

A cramp of terror seizes my heart. As in the worst nightmares, the words seem to take an endless amount of time just to come out of my mouth, whereas the movements of the human beings around me accelerate with dizzying speed. I can sense that Paul will vanish around the door before my words make it into the open air—the air of my salvation, the air of my final redemption. So I move, gesticulate, throw my pillow to the floor and, oh infinite mercy, oh miracle of the gods, oh ineffable relief, they turn to look at me.

"What is it, Uncle?"

In two steps—however do they manage to be so nimble, so quick, I must already be in another world, where they seem to me to be seized by the same frenetic gestures as in the earliest silent films, when actors had the accelerated, jerky gestures of dementia—my nephew is once again within earshot. I hiccup with relief, I can see him go tense with worry, I reassure them with a pitiful gesture while Anna hurries to pick up the pillow.

"Not . . . Lenôtre," I croak, "anything . . . but . . . Lenôtre . . . Not . . . a . . . patisserie . . . I . . . want . . . choux . . . in . . . a . . . plastic . . . bag . . . from . . . Leclerc." I gasp for breath. "Soft . . . choux . . . I . . . want . . . supermarket . . . choux . . ."

And while I penetrate deep into his gaze, filling my own with all the strength of my desire and despair—because this is, for the first time quite literally, a question of life or death—I see that he has understood. I sense it, I know it. He nods, and in his nod a fleeting reminiscence of our former complicity is painfully reborn, with a pain that is joyful, calming. I need no longer speak. As he leaves, almost at a run, I let myself slide into the cottony bliss of memory.

They were waiting for me, in their transparent plastic wrapper. On the wooden display, alongside the wrapped baguettes, whole wheat breads, brioches and flans: the little bags of chouquettes, waiting patiently. Because they'd been tossed there, higgledy-piggledy, with no respect for the art of the patissier who had arranged them lovingly, with plenty of room, on a display in front of the counter; they stuck together at the bottom of the bag, squeezed one against the other like sleeping puppies in the tranquil warmth of the fray. Above all, they had been set all warm and steamy in their final resting place, giving off a decisive steam which, when it condensed on the sides of the wrapper, created an environment conducive to sogginess.

The criteria that go into any great chouquette are those of any self-respecting choux pastry. One must avoid softening and chewiness in equal measure. The consistency of the choux must be neither elastic nor limp, neither brittle nor aggressively dry. Their glory stems from an ability to be tender without being frail, and firm without being stiff. It is incumbent upon patissiers who fill choux with cream to avoid contaminating the filled choux with sogginess. I have already written vengeful and devastating chronicles on those choux that utterly went off the rails, sumptuous pages on the capital importance of borders where *choux à la crème* are concerned—and on bad choux, the ones that can no longer be distinguished from the butter seeping from within, their identity lost in the indolence of a substance to which it should however have opposed the perennial nature of its difference. Or something to that effect.

How can one betray oneself to such a degree? What corruption greater even than power can lead us to thus deny the proof of pleasure, to hold in contempt that which we have loved, to defile our own taste to such a degree? I was fifteen years old, I had just left the lycée for the day, famished the way one often is at that age, without discernment, quite wildly, and yet with a tranquility that I recall only today, and that is precisely what is so cruelly lacking in my entire oeuvre. My entire oeuvre—I would give it all this evening without regret, without a shadow of remorse or a smidgeon of nostalgia, for one single, final chouquette from the supermarket.

I opened the bag carelessly, yanked on the plastic and then tore coarsely at the hole my impatience had created. I thrust my hand into the bag, and I didn't like the sticky contact with the sugar that condensation had left on the sides of the bag. Painstakingly I detached one chouquette from its fellows, carried it religiously to my mouth and swallowed it down, closing my eyes.

Much has been written about the first bite, the second, and the third. Many worthy things have been professed on the subject. All are true. But they do not attain, far from it, the ineffable nature of that sensation, of lightly touching then gradually crushing the moist batter in a mouth that has become orgasmic. The sugar had soaked in moisture and did not crunch; it crystallized as you bit into it, its particles broke up without violence, harmoniously, your jaws did not break the sugar, but scattered it gently, in an indescribable waltz of creamy and crunchy. The chouquette clung to the most secret membranes of my palate, it sensual softness embraced my cheeks, its indecent elasticity caused it to congeal immediately in a homogeneous and unctuous paste which the sweetness of the sugar enhanced with a hint of perfection. I swallowed it quickly, because there were nineteen more to explore. Only the last chouquettes would be chewed and chewed again with the despair of the imminent end. I found consolation in musing about the last offering of the divine little pouch: the crystals of sugar that remained at the very bottom, waiting for choux to cling to: using my sticky fingers, I would fill the last little magical spheres with this sugar, to conclude my feast in an explosion of sweetness.

In the almost mystical union between my tongue and these supermarket chouquettes, with their industrial batter and their treacly sugar, I attained God. Since then, I have lost him, sacrificed him to the glorious desires which were not mine and which, in the twilight of my life, have very nearly succeeded in concealing him from me again.

God—that is, raw, unequivocal pleasure, the pleasure which stems from our innermost core, cares for nothing other than our own delight, and returns to it in like fashion; God—that is, that mysterious region in our most secret self with which we are completely in tune in the apotheosis of authentic desire and unadulterated pleasure. Like the umbilicus nestled in our deepest phantasms, which only our deepest self can inspire, chouquettes were the assumption of my life strength, of my power to exist. I could have written about chouquettes my whole life long; and my whole life long, I wrote against them. It is only in the instant of my death that I have found them again, after so many years of wandering. And it matters little, in the end, whether Paul brings them to me before I expire.

The question is not one of eating, nor is it one of living; the question is knowing why. In the name of the father, the son, and the chouquette, amen. I die.

My thanks to Pierre Gagnaire, for his menu and for his poetry.

ABOUT THE AUTHOR

Muriel Barbery was born in 1969 in Casablanca. She studied philosophy at the Ecole Normale Supérieure and worked for many years as a philosophy teacher in France. Her *New York Times* bestselling novel *The Elegance of the Hedgehog* (Europa Editions 2008) has been published in more than twenty languages. Barbery lives in Japan and is working on a third novel.

www.europaeditions.com

Carmine Abate
Between Two Seas
"A moving portrayal of generational continuity."—*Kirkus*
192 pp • $14.95 • 978-1-933372-40-2

Salwa Al Neimi
The Proof of the Honey
"Al Neimi announces the end of a taboo in the Arab world:
that of sex!"—*Reuters*
160 pp • $15.00 • 978-1-933372-68-6

Alberto Angela
A Day in the Life of Ancient Rome
"Fascinating and accessible."—*Il Giornale*
392 pp • $16.00 • 978-1-933372-71-6

Muriel Barbery
The Elegance of the Hedgehog
"Gently satirical, exceptionally winning and inevitably
bittersweet."—Michael Dirda, *The Washington Post*
336 pp • $15.00 • 978-1-933372-60-0

Stefano Benni
Margherita Dolce Vita
"A modern fable...hilarious social commentary."—*People*
240 pp • $14.95 • 978-1-933372-20-4

Timeskipper
"Benni again unveils his Italian brand of magical realism."—*Library Journal*
400 pp • $16.95 • 978-1-933372-44-0

Massimo Carlotto
The Goodbye Kiss
"A masterpiece of Italian noir."—*Globe and Mail*
160 pp • $14.95 • 978-1-933372-05-1

Death's Dark Abyss
"A remarkable study of corruption and redemption."
—*Kirkus* (starred review)
160 pp • $14.95 • 978-1-933372-18-1

The Fugitive
"[Carlotto is] the reigning king of Mediterranean noir."
—*The Boston Phoenix*
176 pp • $14.95 • 978-1-933372-25-9

Francisco Coloane
Tierra del Fuego
"Coloane is the Jack London of our times."—Alvaro Mutis
176 pp • $14.95 • 978-1-933372-63-1

Giancarlo De Cataldo
The Father and the Foreigner
"A slim but touching noir novel from one of Italy's best writers
in the genre."—*Quaderni Noir*
160 pp • $15.00 • 978-1-933372-72-3

Shashi Deshpande
The Dark Holds No Terrors
"[Deshpande is] an extremely talented storyteller."—*Hindustan Times*
272 pp • $15.00 • 978-1-933372-67-9

Steve Erickson
Zeroville
"A funny, disturbing, daring and demanding novel—Erickson's best."
—*The New York Times Book Review*
352 pp • $14.95 • 978-1-933372-39-6

Elena Ferrante
The Days of Abandonment
"The raging, torrential voice of [this] author is something rare."
—*The New York Times*
192 pp • $14.95 • 978-1-933372-00-6

Troubling Love
"Ferrante's polished language belies the rawness
of her imagery."—*The New Yorker*
144 pp • $14.95 • 978-1-933372-16-7

The Lost Daughter
"So refined, almost translucent."—*The Boston Globe*
144 pp • $14.95 • 978-1-933372-42-6

Jane Gardam
Old Filth
"Old Filth belongs in the Dickensian pantheon of memorable characters."—*The New York Times Book Review*
304 pp • $14.95 • 978-1-933372-13-6

The Queen of the Tambourine
"A truly superb and moving novel."—*The Boston Globe*
272 pp • $14.95 • 978-1-933372-36-5

The People on Privilege Hill
"Engrossing stories of hilarity and heartbreak."—*Seattle Times*
208 pp • $15.95 • 978-1-933372-56-3

Alicia Giménez-Bartlett
Dog Day
"Delicado and Garzón prove to be one of the more engaging sleuth teams to debut in a long time."—*The Washington Post*
320 pp • $14.95 • 978-1-933372-14-3

Prime Time Suspect
"A gripping police procedural."—*The Washington Post*
320 pp • $14.95 • 978-1-933372-31-0

Death Rites
"Petra is developing into a good cop, and her earnest efforts to assert her authority...are worth cheering."—*The New York Times*
304 pp • $16.95 • 978-1-933372-54-9

Katharina Hacker
The Have-Nots
"Hacker's prose soars."—*Publishers Weekly*
352 pp • $14.95 • 978-1-933372-41-9

Patrick Hamilton
Hangover Square
"Patrick Hamilton's novels are dark tunnels of misery, loneliness, deceit, and sexual obsession."—*New York Review of Books*
336 pp • $14.95 • 978-1-933372-06-8

James Hamilton-Paterson
Cooking with Fernet Branca
"Irresistible!"—*The Washington Post*
288 pp • $14.95 • 978-1-933372-01-3

Amazing Disgrace
"It's loads of fun, light and dazzling as a peacock feather."
—*New York Magazine*
352 pp • $14.95 • 978-1-933372-19-8

Rancid Pansies
"Campy comic saga about hack writer and self-styled 'culinary genius' Gerald Samper."—*Seattle Times*
288 pp • $15.95 • 978-1-933372-62-4

Seven-Tenths: The Sea and Its Thresholds
"The kind of book that, were he alive now, Shelley might have written."
—Charles Sprawson
416 pp • $16.00 • 978-1-933372-69-3

www.europaeditions.com

Alfred Hayes
The Girl on the Via Flaminia
"Immensely readable."—*The New York Times*
160 pp • $14.95 • 978-1-933372-24-2

Jean-Claude Izzo
Total Chaos
"Izzo's Marseilles is ravishing."—*Globe and Mail*
256 pp • $14.95 • 978-1-933372-04-4

Chourmo
"A bitter, sad and tender salute to a place equally impossible
to love or leave."—*Kirkus* (starred review)
256 pp • $14.95 • 978-1-933372-17-4

Solea
"[Izzo is] a talented writer who draws from the deep, dark well
of noir."—*The Washington Post*
208 pp • $14.95 • 978-1-933372-30-3

The Lost Sailors
"Izzo digs deep into what makes men weep."
—*Time Out New York*
272 pp • $14.95 • 978-1-933372-35-8

A Sun for the Dying
"Beautiful, like a black sun, tragic and desperate."—*Le Point*
224 pp • $15.00 • 978-1-933372-59-4

Gail Jones
Sorry
"Jones's gift for conjuring place and mood rarely falters."
—*Times Literary Supplement*
240 pp • $15.95 • 978-1-933372-55-6

Matthew F. Jones
Boot Tracks
"A gritty action tale."—*The Philadelphia Inquirer*
208 pp • $14.95 • 978-1-933372-11-2

Ioanna Karystiani
The Jasmine Isle
"A modern Greek tragedy about love foredoomed
and family life."—*Kirkus*
288 pp • $14.95 • 978-1-933372-10-5

Gene Kerrigan
The Midnight Choir
"The lethal precision of his closing punches leave quite a lasting mark."
—*Entertainment Weekly*
368 pp • $14.95 • 978-1-933372-26-6

Little Criminals
"A great story…relentless and brilliant."—Roddy Doyle
352 pp • $16.95 • 978-1-933372-43-3

Peter Kocan
Fresh Fields
"A stark, harrowing, yet deeply courageous work of immense power
and magnitude."—*Quadrant*
304 pp • $14.95 • 978-1-933372-29-7

The Treatment and the Cure
"Kocan tells this story with grace and humor."—*Publishers Weekly*
256 pp • $15.95 • 978-1-933372-45-7

Helmut Krausser
Eros
"Helmut Krausser has succeeded in writing a great
German epochal novel."—*Focus*
352 pp • $16.95 • 978-1-933372-58-7

Amara Lakhous
Clash of Civilizations Over an Elevator in Piazza Vittorio
"Do we have an Italian Camus on our hands? Just possibly."
—*The Philadelphia Inquirer*
144 pp • $14.95 • 978-1-933372-61-7

Carlo Lucarelli
Carte Blanche
"Lucarelli proves that the dark and sinister are better evoked
when one opts for unadulterated grit and grime."
—*The San Diego Union-Tribune*
128 pp • $14.95 • 978-1-933372-15-0

The Damned Season
"De Luca…is a man both pursuing and pursued. And that makes him
one of the more interesting figures in crime fiction."
—*The Philadelphia Inquirer*
128 pp • $14.95 • 978-1-933372-27-3

Via delle Oche
"Delivers a resolution true to the series' moral relativism."
—*Publishers Weekly*
160 pp • $14.95 • 978-1-933372-53-2

Edna Mazya
Love Burns
"Combines the suspense of a murder mystery with the absurdity
of a Woody Allen movie."—*Kirkus*
224 pp • $14.95 • 978-1-933372-08-2

Sélim Nassib
I Loved You for Your Voice
"Nassib spins a rhapsodic narrative out of the indissoluble
connection between two creative souls."—*Kirkus*
272 pp • $14.95 • 978-1-933372-07-5

The Palestinian Lover
"A delicate, passionate novel in which history and life are
inextricably entwined."—*RAI Books*
192 pp • $14.95 • 978-1-933372-23-5

Amélie Nothomb
Tokyo Fiancée
"Intimate and honest…depicts perfectly a nontraditional romance."
—*Publishers Weekly*
160 pp • $15.00 • 978-1-933372-64-8

Alessandro Piperno
The Worst Intentions
"A coruscating mixture of satire, family epic, Proustian meditation,
and erotomaniacal farce."—*The New Yorker*
320 pp • $14.95 • 978-1-933372-33-4

Eric-Emmanuel Schmitt
The Most Beautiful Book in the World
"Nine novellas, parables on the idea of a future, filled with redeeming
optimism."—*Lire Magazine*
192 pp • $15.00 • 978-1-933372-74-7

Domenico Starnone
First Execution
"Starnone's books are small theatres of action, both physical and psychological."—*L'espresso* (Italy)
176 pp • $15.00 • 978-1-933372-66-2

Joel Stone
The Jerusalem File
"Joel Stone is a major new talent."—*Cleveland Plain Dealer*
160 pp • $15.00 • 978-1-933372-65-5

Benjamin Tammuz
Minotaur
"A novel about the expectations and compromises that humans create for themselves."—*The New York Times*
192 pp • $14.95 • 978-1-933372-02-0

Chad Taylor
Departure Lounge
"There's so much pleasure and bafflement to be derived from this thriller."—*The Chicago Tribune*
176 pp • $14.95 • 978-1-933372-09-9

www.europaeditions.com

Roma Tearne
Mosquito
"Vividly rendered…Wholly satisfying."—*Kirkus*
352 pp • $16.95 • 978-1-933372-57-0

Bone China
"Tearne deftly reveals the corrosive effects of civil strife on private lives
and the redemptiveness of art."—*The Guardian*
432 pp • $16.00 • 978-1-933372-75-4

Christa Wolf
One Day a Year: 1960-2000
"Remarkable!"—*The New Yorker*
640 pp • $16.95 • 978-1-933372-22-8

Edwin M. Yoder Jr.
Lions at Lamb House
"Yoder writes with such wonderful manners, learning,
and detachment."—William F. Buckley, Jr.
256 pp • $14.95 • 978-1-933372-34-1

Michele Zackheim
Broken Colors
"A beautiful novel."—*Library Journal*
320 pp • $14.95 • 978-1-933372-37-2